Clandestine

Clandestine

The CIA, a secret partnership, and an
alliance to topple a Government

Stella Francis Faulkes

Rock Creek House, rockcreekhouse.com

For information or to contact the author:

info@rockcreekhouse.com
Printed in the United States of America

ISBN-10:0996510206 (EPUB)
ISBN 978-0-9965102-0-2 (EPUB)
ISBN-10:0996510222 (MOBI)
ISBN-13:978-0-9965102-2-6 (MOBI)
ISBN-10: 0996510214
ISBN-13: 9780996510219
Library of Congress Control Number: 2015911507
Rock Creek Consulting LLC, Twin Falls, Idaho

Cover Illustration Copyright © 2015
Cover design by Augustus Smith, BookFondlers, Inc.

To my husband, Jeff, who brought color
into a black-and-white world.

Introduction

On October 17, 1988, President Reagan awarded the Presidential Medal of Freedom, the highest civilian award, to Irving Brown. The award is presented to individuals who have made especially meritorious contributions to the security or national interests of the United States, to world peace, or to cultural or other significant public or private endeavors.

At the presentation ceremony, the president said: "As the European representative of the American Federation of Labor (AFL) in the late 1940s, Irving Brown played a crucial role in breaking the hold of international communism over postwar Western Europe. By doing so, he can truly be called one of the architects of Western democracy. He has shunned publicity, believing the cause of freedom is far more important than the pleasure of fame. But his modesty cannot obscure the size of his accomplishments, and they have earned Irving Brown the gratitude of his country."

President Reagan stated in his speech that the man had helped stop communism from leaching its way into the unions of post-World War II Europe. Singlehandedly?

The second organized labor representative to receive the honor was John Sweeney, head of the Solidarity Center, a creation of the AFL-CIO. On October 19, 2011, President Obama bestowed on him that same award, the Presidential Medal of Freedom.

The Solidarity Center is something of an enigma. Its funding is derived mainly from the US State Department and the National Endowment for Democracy. In fact, the Solidarity Center receives over 95 percent of its funding from the federal government. Directly from its own web page, the Center describes itself as follows:

> Founded in 1997, the Solidarity Center works with unions, worker associations and community groups worldwide to achieve equitable and sustainable development and to help men and women everywhere stand up for their rights and improve their working and living conditions.

The Solidarity Center operates in sixty countries with twenty-four field offices. It was globalizing long before being global was cool. It was a veritable trendsetter.

The Solidarity Center has not always been called that. Prior to 1997 it went by the name "American Center for International Labor Solidarity," or ACILS, and it was purportedly involved in the attempted coup of the late Venezuelan dictator Hugo Chavez in 2002. The coup, which only temporarily succeeded in removing Chavez, was the result of the matchmaking done by ACILS between the leadership of the conservative, labor-based Confederation of Venezuelan Workers (CTV) and the FEDCAMARAS, an organization of businesses. In addition, the coalition also included some of the leaders of the Catholic Church.

Of course, such benevolence must be funded. The National Endowment for Democracy, or NED, as it is affectionately referred to by its supporters and detractors alike, is a private, nonprofit foundation that describes itself as being dedicated to the growth and strengthening of democratic institutions around the world. Each year NED awards more than a thousand grants to support the projects of nongovernmental groups abroad working for democratic goals in more than ninety countries.

It was founded in 1983 under the Reagan administration and since then has managed to be embroiled in the frontline movements of democratic struggles wherever such struggles might exist.

In countries that have captured American interest, NED is quite an important player. In September 1991, Allen Weinstein commented to the *Washington Post*: "A lot of what we do today was done covertly twenty-five years ago by the CIA." Allen Weinstein was one of those who shaped the legislation that created the foundation.

Through its partnership with the AFL-CIO, NED has been able to target emerging activists in developing countries that are ripe for "assistance" from organizations such as the American Labor Organization, which preaches workers' rights.

NED is not aligned with any particular political party or loyal to any specific political administration in Washington, DC: "By its very nature, such support cannot be governed by the short-term policy preferences of a particular US administration or by the partisan political interests of any party or group." Further, "The Endowment will be effective in carrying out its mission only if it stands apart from immediate policy disputes and represents a consistent, bipartisan, long-term approach to strengthening democracy that will be supported through successive administrations."

NED's importance to US foreign interests exceeds any one man, and because it has the potential to influence governments of other countries, it was designed with the intention of not allowing any US president the ability to roll back its efforts. The NED operates as an NGO—a nongovernmental agency. For an organization that promotes democracy so strenuously, NED seems to operate without any democratic oversight whatsoever. This actually isn't much different from any other NGO or government agency in the United States today. The US Congress funds NED annually through appropriations. The amount of the appropriation has varied year by year, but it has never even been a part of the conversation when Congress discusses cuts in the federal budget. In fact, there are times when Congress has gifted NED with additional funding when countries of specific interest have earned the need for a more specialized program in democracy.

It is by drawing on these facts that I have created the work of fiction that follows.

"The revolution is not an apple that falls when it is ripe;
you have to make it fall"

—CHE GUEVARA

Prologue

September 25th, 2011

Andy Wayne, president of the Association of Retail and Wholesale Workers, sat in his hotel room in Tunisia. The Africa Jade Thalasso in Korba was an excellent location to conduct his business from. It was a clean and very well-run hotel, sitting next to a wonderful stretch of unspoiled beach just north of Nabeul, in Cap Bon. The safari-inspired interior design, with caged birds in the lobby and ceilings painted with scenes from the African Savannah, stayed on just the right side of kitsch. The gardens were well kept, and there were trees and birds populating the open courtyards between the rooms, which was charming.

The staff was professional and helpful. The hotel's restaurant, Restaurant Jade, was a delightful setting for an evening meal, and the food was decent. The snack café near the pool was a bit disorganized, but friendly enough. The rooms were fine, the pool large. The beach was clean, with silver sand stretching in each direction. The bar down on the beach was smart and funky—an attractive spot from which to survey the sea. It was in places like this that Andy could almost forget the darker side of what he did for a living. But then this was the balance that one must seek when one had a darker side. Andy was there to guide a new labor movement. But it was not the first time he had been there.

The Tunisian revolution was the first shot fired in what would later be called the Arab Spring. It was an intense crusade of popular resistance, including a series of street demonstrations that erupted across the Tunisian landscape. Labor unions were an integral part of the protests, as they had been in the short-lived overthrow of Hugo Chavez in Venezuela. The protests inspired similar actions throughout the Arab world. The events began on December 18, 2010, and eventually led to the ousting of long-time President Zine El Abidine Ben Ali in January 2011, leading to a thorough democratization of the country and to free and democratic elections that saw the victory of a coalition of the Islamist Ennahda movement with the center-left Congress for the Republic and the left-leaning Ettakatol as junior partners.

The protests were sparked by the self-immolation of Mohamed Bouazizi in December 2010 and led to the ousting of President Zine El Abidine Ben Ali twenty-eight days later, when he officially resigned after bolting to Saudi Arabia, concluding twenty-three years in power. The revolt in Tunisia was unexpected in most of the world, but not by the Board. The Board, as it was called by those who worked for the Center for Labor Unity, or CLU, included a very select, very secret cabal of people. The Board had known that it would upset the Middle East applecart, but the world's feathers needed a little ruffling. US interests as well as a one-world government objective were at stake, and the best place to start the facade of democracy was with the labor organizations. It was the door that always opened to outside influence. It was an easier way to spread democracy than actually invading countries, like President George W. Bush did in Iraq.

Those who sat on the Board directly reflected the countries that were members of NATO. Each NATO country had one representative. The Board had been formed by NATO shortly after its own creation. At that time, member countries recognized that there needed to be an organization that operated above the pedestrian politics of each country—a group that relentlessly pursued a common goal of world order and peace. In the beginning it was designed to prevent another world war from ever taking place; in the end it became more proactive in creating a world that the group felt should exist, with NATO as the central policing organization as well as its governing body through proxy governments set up in countries who currently did not see things the same way as the Board. The Board had rivals in Russia and China, however. Those two countries would never unite. They satisfied their need for allies through third-world puppet regimes.

The Board was more aggressive in pursuing its agenda— an agenda that was normally communicated to CLU through a phone call from the Board's COO, whose real identity remained hidden, or, more commonly, through one Ezekiel Jones, who chose to make his presence known more often than not in person.

Andy was now there to make sure that the labor unions formed a tighter bond with the American labor organizations, a solidarity that would withstand any outside infiltrations of Muslim extremist organizations like the Muslim Brotherhood. It was a tradition that the American AFL-CIO had been carrying out since World War II, when the forerunner of the AFL-CIO, the AFL combined resources with the CIA to keep communism from infiltrating the European unions as they rebuilt after World War II. It was a partnership, a clandestine union between US unions and the CIA that had been forged over decades.

Wayne, an influential union leader in New York City, was in Tunisia, advising the fledgling labor movement there, when he received a flood of phone calls and e-mails warning him about the beginnings of a movement back home. That was never good, Andy thought.

Wayne called a colleague of his in Washington, DC, to inquire about this new "uprising in the States," but he only got a vague description of what was happening. Was it just a bunch of hippies, druggies, or young assholes with too much time on their hands? His buddy didn't know. Would the movement fade fast? Die out? Again, the response left the initial question unanswered. Thus alerted to the spreading protests, Andy Wayne received a call a couple of days later from Koshka Whitehall.

Koshka was the product of a Russian immigrant and a man who could trace his lineage back to the first English colonist; she was also the head of the CLU. "Koshka" meant "cat" in Russian, so her staff christened her with the nickname Miss Kitty. Of course, they only referred to her by that name when she was not present. Andy Wayne actually had many names for her, depending on the disposition of their relationship at the time and his frame of mind. Icy Hot was one of his favorites. The moniker applied to her physical attributes, not her disposition. She was Nordic pale in complexion, and her hair was various shades of blond with icy white strands intermingled with golden ones. Her eyes were a bright, icy blue. She looked like an ice queen, but she made every male hot from just seeing her. Should they have the misfortune of actually meeting her, however, they would find a personality with all the warmth of a glacier. She was forty-five but looked ten years younger.

She said little when she called. She seldom said much over the phone anyway, even ones that were secured. She simply told him that he was needed. Of course, he made travel arrangements immediately. He would be flying out tomorrow. The Arab spring would have to get along without him for now.

In the coming weeks, several powerful unions would make their major push to join forces with the Occupy Wall Street movement. The newspapers quoted Andy Wayne as saying, "The organized labor effort needs to capture the vitality and drive of the Occupy Wall Street movement and learn from them. They have impacted a nation and are reaching our country's people on a level not seen before. This is electrifying a lot of the people whom the labor movement has been fighting to reach for years."

The AFL-CIO powers intervened in the Occupy Wall Street protests to prevent them from evolving into a mass rebellion independent of the "US" government and in favor of socialism—or even dissolving into anarchy. Nothing horrified the kingpins of labor more than the rumor of a youth or working-class revolt in the United States.

The US government, equally anxious to see the political crushing of the Occupy Wall Street movement, came to the conclusion that the involvement of the AFL-CIO in the Wall Street protests was the preferable method for controlling the results. The first name that Koshka came up with was Andy Wayne's. At this point some of those active in the socialist movement in the United States were asking who—or what—was Andy Wayne.

What was Mr. Wayne doing in Tunisia? The mainstream media did not say. Actually, it didn't even manage to investigate, let alone do a story on why organized labor was in Tunisia before and after the revolution. The general framework of the AFL-CIO intervention there through CLU was clear, based on the organization's history with the CIA and the CLU's recent activity. Besides, the media, for the most part, sympathized with organized labor, so it never troubled itself to look too closely at its activities.

In any case, it would be a miscalculation of Andy Wayne's industrious nature to refer only to this specific Tunisian endeavor. His talents and accomplishments were far more wide-ranging. Mr. Wayne was a busy man.

Andy Wayne was "breathtakingly" handsome, according to some women. He was accomplished and, in the eyes of the world, quite successful at the relatively young age of forty-one. He was tall—at least six foot four. Although he was not given to physical exercise, his physique was lean and muscular, with broad shoulders. He sported a thick head of dark, mahogany hair that was just starting to hint at gray around the temples. A neatly trimmed beard framed a strong jaw, and a mustache accented full lips. His dark brown eyes shifted quickly from warm and comical to black and intense. As well as serving as the youngest president of the hundred-thousand-member Association of Retail and Wholesale Workers (ARWW), now a division of the Commercial Workers Union, Wayne was president of the David Alliance Committee, a pro-Israeli lobby within the American trade unions. In this position, he repeatedly promoted Israeli policy, although in its more "moderate" Labor Party form, and censured Palestinian opposition.

Wayne also functioned as one of the junior vice president of the national AFL-CIO, where he had been a member of the organization's executive council from 2001 until 2007. He currently served as a vice president of the Maryland State AFL-CIO and the Baltimore City Central Labor Council.

He also played a prominent role in the Democratic party, having served formerly as chief house counsel of the party's national committee.

The ARWW president also found time to sit on the board of trustees of Liberty Community, a Washington, DC, institution most closely associated with CIA-directed anticommunist literature during the Cold War against the Soviet Union and the other Stalinist regimes. Famous political activists Naomi Carter and Edison Sherman, in their *Modern Manifesto* (1989), noted that Liberty Community "interlaces" with various US governmental bodies such as Radio Free Europe and the CIA. It "has long served," they wrote, "as an effective propaganda appendage of the government and international left wing."

Wayne sat on the Liberty Community board with a variety of academics, trade-union officials, and assorted US government operatives, past and present. Another Liberty Community trustee was the wife of an attaché to the embassy in Honduras during the 1980s who played a key role in supplying and supervising the CIA-backed "contra" mercenaries who were based in that country.

Another member of the board was the undersecretary of state for democracy and global affairs from 2004 to 2008. Charles Jordain, former undersecretary, also belonged to the executive council of the Trust for Security of Fairness (TSF), a one-world think tank set up after 9/11 to combat Islamic fundamentalism.

The affiliation with TSF brought Andy into the social circle of billionaire Max Plow, a former FBI director, a retired congressman, a former Senate leader, former national security adviser, and a former CIA deputy director.

These were the shadowy realms and lofty circles in which Andy Wayne lived and breathed. What he would bring to the Occupy Wall Street protesters was a calculatingly charming personality guided by the strategic dictates of CLU to disarm and gut the Occupy movement. After all, it just wouldn't do to have the country whose government held the lead position on the Board in favor of a one-world governing body to face its own revolution. That would throw into question the whole viability of using democracy as the method for ushering in a global leadership.

One

Present Day

During the Arab spring, the rebellion that started in Tunisia spread quickly to Libya and exploded into Egypt. While Tunisia, which had the full attention of the CLU and had been finessed skillfully by Andy Wayne, was exhibiting calm as the country transitioned into a full-fledged democracy, in Egypt the journey to democracy was not going as expected.

Out of all the countries, Egypt was the one where the Board expected the fewest problems. After decades of religious tolerance and a popular military that was best buds with the American military, Egypt was the last place anyone expected the Muslim Brotherhood to win a democratic election. That put the brakes on continuing the Arab spring through Yemen and Syria. In Yemen it was relatively easy to put the revolution genie back in the bottle, but in Syria it turned into a veritable crisis of indecision. It was all but impossible to backpedal out of it. Unfortunately, that is exactly what the president and his trusted advisors attempted to do, and that in turn opened the door to a crowd of garden-variety extremists, who jumped in to lend the Syrian rebels a hand.

Luckily for the United States, Russia, which was originally going to offer Assad asylum, was able to pivot into offering military aid, which was how the Syrian dictator was able to hold his own in the fight. Of course, this could also be viewed as bad news, as there were those who believed that Russia was working to undermine the United States' dominant role in the move toward one-world governance.

Libya was experiencing the same hiccups that came with forming a new democracy, but with the exception of the massacre of embassy staff by Islamist extremists, all was quiet. That was a dark tale of its own; Libya correctly identified the attack as a terrorist attack while the State Department continued to embarrass itself, displaying its inability to smoothly cover for what had been really happening under the guise of embassy business. Worried that by admitting it was a terrorist attack, it would then be required to explain why the attack happened under an administration that had prematurely issued the obituary of Al-Qaeda, it retreated behind a storyline that gave new meaning to the word "fable."

In the minds of most Americans, terrorists were irrational beings at best, with no rhyme or reason to the violence they perpetuated, and had been accepted as a permanent, if not welcome, addition to the world stage.

Egypt, however, should not have gone down the road it did. But the elections were held prematurely, not allowing for the more moderate groups to consolidate, which gave way to a Muslim extremist being elected. Once in, the general opinion was to step back and see what road Morsi would take them down.

Unfortunately, the road was one of intolerance and Sharia law. That could not be allowed to continue, so an impromptu military coup was staged so that there could be a rerun on the elections. The Board should have known Egypt would be trouble when, in February of 2011, it cracked down on pro-democracy and rights groups. That crackdown netted the Egyptian government sixteen Americans—Americans who appeared to have a loose connection to CLU—as well as eleven other rights workers from countries including Serbia and England who also had connections to purported labor organizations from their own countries.

Kamal el-Ganzouri, the military-backed prime minister, said his country would not halt the crackdown despite what he called threats to cut off aid. But of course they backed off after the United States padded their pockets with five million dollars in bail money. Soon after, that June, Mohammed Morsi was elected, and it all went to hell. Now a second military coup. And yes, it was a military coup of sorts that ousted Mubarak in the first place.

Two

Koshka was sitting at her desk when Andy entered her office. She was totally absorbed in whatever it was she was studying on her computer screen. She barely glanced up. She had aged little since 2011. Tunisia and Occupy Wall Street were in her rearview mirror. Koshka was not one to go back; she always moved forward. Her group had done its job. The rest was someone else's responsibility, and she wasn't one to revisit someone else's failure, even if it did destroy the groundwork her people had put in.

Today, CLU's attention was focused back on South America. With the death of Hugo Chavez and Raul Castro stepping away from his brother Fidel's policies, the Latin countries were now back in play. It was the habit of the committee to rotate between countries and continents anyway. Not too long ago, at a time when economic turmoil and austerity measures reared their ugly heads in many countries, Brazil received well-deserved recognition for its successes in lifting nearly forty million of its citizens out of extreme poverty over the past ten years while fostering economic expansion for the nation. During that time, CLU, as well as the US government, had cemented their bonds with the people of Brazil. This opened the door to being able to get cooperation from them when any effort was underway in South America. Fortunately, the Brazilians were very astute and realized that a partnership with the Americans benefited them on many levels.

A well-attended brown-bag discussion at the AFL-CIO this week had provided background on Brazil's transformation, insights about the work needed to continue improving conditions for Brazilian workers, and food for thought about the example Brazil had set for the United States and the world.

"The Center For Labor Unity in Brazil is working on a number of fronts," Koshka said as she glanced at the paperwork in front of her.

Out of the blue, she posed a couple of questions to Andy. "Do you think they do any exorcisms in the US anymore? I mean, you never hear about demons or houses that are possessed—that sort of thing. Maybe they just don't talk about it anymore. I don't know, where do you think demons and hauntings have gone in the US?"

"Planning a family reunion, Koshka? Looking for some long-lost relatives?" Andy was used to her strange, out-of-context comments. Usually they were the byproduct of something that she had read or experienced that her mind was still toying with.

She glanced up long enough to shoot him an icy glare. "No, I saw that movie *The Conjuring* this weekend. It was quite good, and I was just thinking about the circumstances the movie was based on."

"Well, perhaps all our demons are in the Middle East. That would be a hotbed of excitement for a demon. All that blood-lust and evil miasma that hangs over that region. They are all probably members of the Muslim Brotherhood. No chance of a pesky Catholic exorcism there."

She remained silent for a moment.

"Andy, I need you in South America. We have an excellent opportunity there to start moving that region toward the Board's goal."

"My prayers have been answered. Hot, sultry Latina women, tropical locale. How do I explain this to the labor union that I am supposedly leading—the Association of Retail and Wholesale Workers? You do remember them, don't you? What do I tell my members that their fearless leader is doing?"

"Well, Andrew, maybe you can just tell them that you are down there to try to organize the sweatshops created by the designer garment industries? Perhaps that old standby—leveling the playing field—will work. For God's sake, Wayne, you act like the working class has an IQ that actually registers on the scale. If they had any form of intellect at all, do you think they would be called 'working class'? Or sucked into some warped sense of equality through collectivism?"

She sat back in her chair. "Honestly, sometimes I think you really believe you're leading some workers' liberation front. You're not the savior of the unwashed masses. There is us, and there is them. We take care of them through social programs because they are unable to take care of themselves. It's probably a flaw in their breeding—something in the genetics. We march with them; make all the right noises to let them think we are with them, and then we retreat to our gated—and well-deserved—upscale living environments. Good God, if they had a brain, they would realize that as we stand there, chanting beside them about redistribution of wealth and all that BS, we haven't once voluntarily redistributed our wealth. What morons. Look at the star-studded actors and celebrities who champion their cause while they cavort in a gilded society protected by bodyguards. Don't any of these 'working class' ever wonder why their much-worshipped rock stars never offer to share their accumulated wealth? People that stupid deserve to be controlled. It's better for them in the long run."

Her distaste for the subject matter showed on her face. No one could accuse Koshka of empathy. In fact, Koshka subscribed to a quasi-communistic form of government. She felt the problem with the old USSR was that they controlled people in areas they shouldn't have. Like travel. The trick was to control them without their knowing they were being controlled. Give the masses food, cell phones, and HDTVs, and you could inflict any type of government on them you chose. Just like the handling of immigration.

The intent of the Board was to create a one-world governing body and two classes of people: a working class and a modern-day aristocracy. To do that you needed to eliminate the middle class and drive down the wages. Immigrants traditionally worked for less, whether it was the Irish in the 1800s or the Mexican immigrants of today. Farmers and construction companies knew this. Why raise the wages so that an American would take the job when you could lower the wages and an immigrant would take the job? Then you defended the allowance of a flood of immigrants by stating that no American would take the job. Of course not. Wages were substandard and kept that way by allowing unskilled immigrants to flood into the country. Even Cesar Chavez acknowledged this, which is why he and his followers often used physical violence on Mexicans coming across the river to do work in the fields. It was Cesar Chavez who coined the term "wetback."

By lowering the wage standards in the United States and lowering the expectations regarding the living standard, you minimize the United States as a superpower. And the United States must not be seen as a superpower if there is to be a one-world order. As a superpower, the United States would only be seen as a conqueror, not as a partner, which is how the countries in the EU see one another. So therefore, the power of the United States and the living standards her citizens enjoy has to be diminished. She could no longer be exceptional.

Andy got up from his seat on the soft black leather sofa.

"Where are you going?" Koshka asked.

"I'm going across the room to your well-stocked bar. I think I need some refreshment after that passionate plea on behalf of the unwashed masses."

"It's a little early to be drinking, isn't it?"

"Oh, I don't know, Koshka. You seemed to bring out the need for whiskey in a man. I'm surprised that Jack Daniels hasn't tapped you for its next spokesperson. One sixty-second plug from you, and I'd imagine the entire world would want to find their way to the bottom of a red-labeled bottle. Perhaps the theme song could be George Thurgood's 'I Drink Alone.' Tell me—just between you and me—is the only family who will hang out with you your dear ol' granddad?"

"Andy, please remember, I have gelded horses. A man can't be that much different."

Andy raised his freshly poured Jack in salute to her. "The riddle of why you are still single has finally been solved."

After a monument of silence, Andy asked, "So am I heading to Brazil?"

It would have been much easier to send Andy directly to Caracas, but when it was revealed that CLU, in concert with the CIA, had been behind the failed coup of Hugo Chavez in 2002, the Venezuelan dictator was quick to kick the CLU out of the country; and the ban was still in place, even though the despot was dead. So Andy's work in the country would have to be done through other channels with the help of an operative in Brazil.

As he waited for Koshka's reply, her assistant, Agnes, buzzed her on the phone's intercom.

"Yes?"

"Mr. Jones is here to see you, Ms. Whitehall," the disembodied voice announced.

"Thank you. Please send him in."

The always dapper and debonair Ezekiel Jones strode into the room with a charming smile affixed to his face.

"I hope I am not interrupting anything?" he cheerfully questioned, although in truth he didn't much care if he was.

"No. Andy was just getting ready to leave. He has much to do before winging his way to South America," Koshka stated while organizing some paperwork on her desk. Her displeasure with Andy was still evident.

"Ah," Ezekiel acknowledged. Then, with his charming smile still in place, his voice became somewhat suggestive as he added, "Please say hi to Joyia for me. She is always, shall we say, passionate about her work."

Andy nodded an acknowledgment to Ezekiel as he rose, placed his now-empty whiskey tumbler on the table, and made his way out of Koshka's office.

"Lovers' quarrel?" Ezekiel asked. Having felt the tension in the room, he was being deliberately provocative. He liked getting under other people's skin, especially Koshka's. It gave him a perverse pleasure to irritate her.

Koshka leaned back in her chair, shifting her gaze from her desk to the man sitting on the other side of it.

"Ezekiel, to what do I owe the pleasure of your visit today?"

"Cuba," was the one-word reply. Ezekiel rubbed his hands together and leaned forward in his chair. "Cuba appears to be open to our tender courtship."

Koshka let out a very unladylike snort. "Cuba may be looking for a date, Ezekiel, but I'm afraid I'm all tapped out of appropriate suitors. Perhaps you haven't noticed, but CLU is spread a little thin right now. We haven't even gotten a street demonstration off in Venezuela, let alone a populist revolution. I cannot see how we'd be able to do anything effective there."

"Koshka, darling, you sadly underestimate your operational skills." Ezekiel leaned back into the chair, stretching his long legs in front of him.

"No, you overestimate them," Koshka rejoined.

Ezekiel studied her for a minute as his charming smile slowly faded. He looked around Koshka's office, his eyes coming to rest on a portrait of Jay Lovestone. Lovestone, the original infiltrator used by George Meany and the CIA in a post-World War II Europe. The once-enthusiastic communist party member turned pro-democracy warrior once promised to rid the world of communism. Beside him was Irving Brown, his partner in crime, so to speak. The two of them had divided and conquered Europe in the United States' fight to keep communism from gaining control of the European unions as they rebuilt after the war. They marked the start of the alliance between the CIA and what was the AFL was at the time, as it had not yet merged with the CIO to form what was now known as the AFL-CIO. George Meany was the captain of that ship. The cigar-chomping, blue-collar labor leader was a zealous anticommunist activist. Beneath the pictures of the two men was a copy of a letter penned by Meany:

The silent partnership

When we think of the historic struggles and conflicts of the current and past century, we naturally think of famous leaders: men who governed nations, commanded armies, and inspired movements in the defense of liberty, or in the service of ideologies which have obliterated liberty. Yet today, in this hour of human history, when the forces arrayed against the free spirit of man are more powerful, more brutal, and potentially more deadly than ever before, the single figure who has raised the highest flame of liberty heads no state, commands no army, and leads no movement that our eyes can see.

But there is a movement—a hidden movement of human beings who have no offices and no headquarters— who are not represented in the great halls where nations meet, who every day risk or suffer more for the right to speak, to think, and to be true to themselves than any of us here are likely to risk in our lifetime.

We heed this voice, not because it speaks for the left or the right or for any faction, but because it hurls truth and courage into the teeth of total power when it would be so much easier and more comfortable to submit to and embrace the lies by which that power lives.

Ezekiel returned his attention to the woman before him. "Koshka." His hand gestured to the framed photos. "Two men were able to beat back the red hordes from taking over the European unions. In fact, one was even awarded the Congressional Medal of Freedom for his efforts. Now with the manpower you have, you are unable to deal with two third-world countries?"

Koshka studied the portraits of the two men that Ezekiel's hand had indicated.

"The world was a much different place then, Ezekiel." She paused for emphasis. "And I am taking on more than two third-world countries."

"It was harder, Koshka. No Internet, no YouTube, and Twitter was something a bird did. Look, funds coming into Cuba from Russia are minimal, and Cuba is worried, with good reason. The Russian economy is in tatters, but who knows how long that will last. This window may only be open for a short period of time. Besides, it would tie in with our plans for Venezuela as it is one of Cuba's biggest supporters, especially with shipping them cheap oil."

Ezekiel steepled his fingers in front of his face as Koshka thought over his words.

"Let me see what I can rearrange," she said. "I just can't move my people around without thinking through the repercussions."

Ezekiel smiled. He knew Koshka well enough to know she was stalling, but he would indulge her for the moment.

"Excuse me now, Ezekiel. I have to put out a press release to give Andy some cover on his upcoming trip to Brazil."

"Koshka, never forget who you work for." Ezekiel addressed her lack of respect.

Ezekiel rose from the chair with a languid grace and left her alone in her office. His steps never made a sound as he crossed the room. Koshka's name may have meant cat, but Ezekiel moved like one. Graceful, quiet, creepy.

The next day, on the CLU website under press releases, Koshka released the following statement:

I am pleased to have the occasion today to announce that Andy Wayne will be representing the Center for Labor Unity in a meeting with the President of Brazil. The president's views on globalization, the Free Trade Area of the Americas (FTAA), and world trade ran parallel with many of the fears of the working men and women in the United States, especially in the retail and garment industry. His suggestions for sensible progress, increased work for our citizens, decent employment, and added social and economic equality create a plan that America's labor organizations can support.

Mr. Wayne will be discussing a number of shared fears and interests, including the reliability of social security systems and government-sponsored retirement programs, trade and workers' rights, and the rights of Brazilian workers in the United States.

They will also be celebrating the camaraderie between the Brazilian labor movement and organized labor in the United States as well as the alliance that labor has enjoyed with the president of Brazil and the Brazilian people. I am honored that, other than the president of the United States and US cabinet members, CLU is the only US organization to have the chance to meet with the president of Brazil during talks on the free trade pact.

Koshka sat back at her desk and read over the press release. Sometimes she wondered why she bothered with this. No one read the website anyway. Those who did were crackpots and conspiracy theorists who were discredited before they could even start a sentence. Ezekiel insisted on this, though. He believed that the devil was in the details, and although Americans might not give it a passing glance, their enemies might be reading it daily.

She walked over to her bar and poured two fingers of whiskey. Her eyes rested on the portrait of George Meany and wondered what he would think of a woman and a communist running what was his brainchild. He would probably want to fire her as he did Jay Lovestone in the 1970s when he found out that the enterprising Lovestone was answering to the CIA more than he was to Mr. Meany. No, she thought, the portly brash bulldog would probably want to tar and feather her. He hated communists. Firing would have been too good for her in his eyes. She was sure that Ezekiel felt the same way about her.

"The tree of liberty needs to be watered with the blood of patriots every now and then," Ezekiel would often spout to justify what was often a bloody outcome to their spreading of democracy. It was all about power, she thought. Liberty be damned, and likewise Ezekiel Jones. "Here's mud in your eye, George," she said softly to the empty room as she toasted George Meany's portrait and then slammed the whiskey back.

Three

Andy flew into the Boa Vista–Atlas Brasil Cantanhede International Airport on TAM Brazilian Airlines. He couldn't find an American airline that flew to the small city by the Amazon. His sixteen-hour flight started out in Orlando, Florida, and had a quick stopover in Sao Paulo before making the final flight into Boa Vista. Unlike foreign operatives who had to infiltrate the metropolises of other countries under assumed names and nationalities, Andy enjoyed the privilege of full disclosure. He never had to hide who he was or switch out a passport.

In fact, just the opposite was true. It was very important for everyone to know that Andy Wayne, labor activist, was there. His past and his picture were readily available online. In Brazil, his arrival was a guaranteed positive event. The friendly relations that had been established between the government of Brazil and the United States, as well as the easy alliance among the officials of CUT and the AFL-CIO, made his welcome assured. Central Única dos Trabalhadores (Unified Workers' Central), commonly known as CUT, was the largest national trade-union organization in Brazil. CUT, formed on August 28,

1983, in São Bernardo do Campo, São Paulo, was no stranger to revolutions and resistance. Alongside the Workers' Party (PT) and the Landless Workers' Movement (MST), CUT was one of the key organizations to challenge the two-decade-old military rule of Brazil by launching massive strikes.

Today, CUT was not only the largest and most important trade-union federation in Brazil; it was the largest trade union in Latin America and the fifth largest in the world. CUT generally supported a democratic socialist political ideology and was close to its brethren in the US Labor Coalition despite also having a strong alliance with the socialist Workers' Party and its leaders, many of whom had been union leaders in the past.

Much like his predecessor, Jay Lovestone, Andy owed his job with the union and his standing in elevated social circles to the CIA, not a union past. It had provided a lucrative career and, at times, a thoroughly satisfying hedonistic lifestyle. He reflected on his luck in landing such a plum position as his plane touched down in Brazil's most remote city.

Boa Vista was the capital of the state of Roraima in the north of Brazil. The city was linked with the other regions of Brazil by air alone, but it could be reached by road through Manaus, capital of the state of Amazonas, and by the city of Bonfim, in Guyana. Boa Vista was the only Brazilian capital located above the equator, and it was a gateway for ecotourism to the Amazon, Venezuela, Guyana, and Suriname, situated on the western bank of the River Branco, 136 miles from Brazil's border with Venezuela.

Boa Vista enjoyed a tropical climate complete with heat and humidity. It was a green city, fringed with leafy mango trees and other lush foliage that thrived in a tropical region. Its main tourist attraction was the beaches situated on the banks of the River Branco, close to the Macuxi Bridge.

Boa Vista was a planned city, but because of its geographical location, far away from the country's major urban centers, it had a small population. Thanks to urban development in the 1960s, it was a modern, level city, designed in the form of a fan, with the broad spokes of wide, woody, tree-lined streets that came together on the Civic Centre square.

One of the most anticipated activities that Andy would engage in was renewing his acquaintance with Joyia Gabriella, his labor contact from CUT. Lord, if only all his contacts could look like and act like her. The sensuous Brazilian was of mixed heritage. Her father was French and her mother Brazilian. Of all the nationalities God chose to combine! Lord have mercy! Andy often felt that just watching her walk into a room was a pornographic experience. Her long hair was thick, glossy, and black, and she had the most startling amber eyes. When the sunlight hit them just right, they almost looked neon. Of course, her thickly accented English turned him on just by listening to it.

Brazil definitely was a positive turn of fortune from Tunisia, although the accommodations couldn't measure up to the Africa Jade Thalasso. One would think that the hotel in Brazil, just by virtue of the country it was located in, would be a huge improvement over anything to be found on the

African continent. A faint smile appeared on his face as he contemplated his stereotyping. It was easy to think of the world from an American point of view and forget that Tunisia was a popular tourist destination for Europeans and just across the water from Italy, which of course would inspire more upscale accommodations.

Once Andy had retrieved his luggage from the carousel, he sauntered out into the sultry South American afternoon. He had no trouble flagging a taxi. Again, the petty pleasure of knowing that he could openly travel while promoting a surreptitious agenda passed through his mind and made him feel giddy inside.

After a short two-and-a-half-mile trip from the airport, the cab stopped in front of the Aipana Plaza Hotel on Praça do Centro Cívico, across from Boa Vista's Centro Cívico square. The reception area of Boa Vista's fanciest hotel had leather sofas, modern paintings, sculptures, and a hip lobby bar. The rooms were no less classy, with muted decor, slate floors, glass showers, comfortable beds, and, most importantly, air conditioning. The rooms also had the added conveniences of cable TV and a minibar. He always chose a room with a view of the pool so that he could gaze at the scantily clad women who lounged lazily by the crystal-blue chlorinated water.

The pool was located by a sumptuous tropical garden that contained mango and coconut trees, which made it a nice escape from the heat. Along with a contemporary bar, the hotel offered a popular restaurant known for its international and regional specialties. Andy's room was spacious, but what he enjoyed most was loafing by the hotel's private pool, cocooned by the lush garden. Along with the quaint poolside bar, which served him the perfect ice-cold beer, a hot day (in Boa Vista, all days were hot) became an indulgent holiday.

On Saturdays, the restaurant offered the best feijoada (fay-ZHWA-dah) in town. This was another of those big, hearty, meat-and-bean stews that seemed to be the national dish of one country or another. In this case, the country was Brazil. Feijoada had as many versions as there were cooks, but in Brazil it almost always had black beans and a mixture of salted, smoked, and fresh meats. Some versions were a little spicy from the sausages; others were totally mild. Some people's feijoada versions were thick, "eat-it-with-a-fork" versions; others, like this one, were more like a traditional stew. Either way, it was traditional to serve this stew with white rice and maybe some sautéed collard greens.

It was one of Andy's favorite dishes whenever he visited. The restaurant was a very popular local "see and be seen" place. Still, the hotel rated only maybe three stars in Andy's book of traveling accommodations. Had there been anything better, he would have dropped his suitcase there instead.

Once Andy had situated himself in his room, he opened the briefing that had been passed to him at the airport in Sao Paulo. The CIA liaison who had slipped it into Andy's messenger bag while he was in the men's room was someone Andy had recognized from a previous encounter in South America. That time, Andy was down there to galvanize a movement to remove Hugo Chavez from power. It had failed.

What caused CLU to move once again into Venezuela was that its government had quietly seized control of two oil rigs owned by a unit of Houston-based Lone Star Energy Suppliers after the company had shut them down because the state oil monopoly was months behind on payments.

While the late President Hugo Chavez liked to grandstand on national television, ordering troops to seize everything from supermarkets to foreign-owned oil companies, his hand-picked successor, Miguel Gomez, had avoided any additional expropriations six months into his rule.

Instead, even while attacking the country's business elite for allegedly hoarding toilet paper and other basic goods as part of an "economic war," he'd insisted Venezuela was open for investment and was seeking to boost production of oil that accounted for 95 percent of exports.

Oil companies were weary of working with PDVSA, the state owned oil and gas company, which had accumulated huge debts to service contractors on whom it depended to develop its proven oil reserves.

Lone Star stopped servicing PDVSA in July, after negotiations broke down over millions of dollars in unpaid bills stretching back to December. Lone Star was a publicly traded oil services company with more than thirty thousand employees worldwide and $34.5 billion in annual revenue.

The current dispute over oil rigs in Venezuela demonstrated that not all the risks of oil drilling were environmental. On June 11, the Venezuelan government seized fourteen rigs from Petroguard, an American drilling services firm. The

Louisiana-based company had stopped production at the rigs and said that Venezuela's PDVSA owed it about $43 million.

Venezuela's late leader, Hugo Chavez, had nationalized many of his nation's oil facilities when he took power. Any company still operating in Venezuela faced some risk of losing assets to the government, but this risk might threaten some firms more than others. The risk profile of each firm depended on its particular relationship with the PDVSA and the government. Some firms actively sought growth and committed resources in Venezuela, whereas other companies were reluctant to put up with the political volatility.

Gomez, who faced legislative elections in September, was following in the steps of his predecessor by pushing ahead with radical plans during election campaigns. Soon after seizing the American-owned drilling rigs, Gomez reached out and seized another US-based corporation's property. Tucked in the business section of the *Wall Street Journal* was an article reporting the most recent transgression against American interests:

CARACAS, Venezuela (FNC)—Venezuela temporarily seized a food-making plant Friday belonging to US-based bakery giant Gourmet Baker, mentioning a production allowance clash.

Venezuelan President Miguel Gomez's government took over a Gourmet Baker plant for the third time in recent months.

Raul Cortez, Venezuela's deputy minister for food, announced the takeover live on the state-run Venezolana de Television channel. He said the plant did not meet production levels for bread sold at lower, government-mandated prices.

An inspection of the plant Thursday found that 47 percent of its bread met the government-established level, Cortez said at a news conference in front of the food plant. Fifty-three percent was "out of regulation," he alleged.

The Venezuelan government will take over the plant for 90 days, he said, and then will determine what steps to take next.

Funny how little had changed, even with the new Venezuelan president. Of course, the new president was nothing more than a clone of the departed Chavez, whose death Andy had saluted with a glass of excellent Prosecco and a New York fashion-model wannabe in his bed. Miguel Gomez had served in the military with Chavez and was instrumental in restoring him to power during that two-week attempted overthrow. The man practically grew to adulthood with his head in Chavez's anal cavity. It would not have surprised Wayne if Gomez had secretly brought Chavez's coffin into his bedroom so he could feel close to the man he had worshipped like a god.

While Andy reviewed the file and waited for the ever-tantalizing and surprisingly intelligent (Andy did not generally like intelligent women, as they tended to require too much work) Joyia Gabriella to make her appearance, another man on another continent was also plotting, but it wasn't a government he wanted to destroy.

Four

Barnard Christophe was in his second term as president of the United States. He was a man without much of a moral compass. His coarse personality and unorthodox viewpoints were hidden behind a brilliant facade of warmth and charisma while in the public eye. His very existence as a second-term president could be attributed to his overwhelming paranoia and his genuine belief that some of his political enemies were evildoers. To overcome these enemies, he felt that he needed to use any political weapon at his disposal to secure his place as president, with no regard to the legality of such measures.

Barnard also believed that as president of the United States, he was permitted to break some of the laws and that he was immune from inquiry. Each of these traits alone was not uncommon in other politicians and world leaders; however, when paired with his cunning charm and mental acuity, the combination was lethal to his political opponents.

Well into his second term now, Barnard was frequently dogged by his persona and the public's perception of it. Editorial cartoonists and comedians often exaggerated his appearance and mannerisms, to the point where the line between the human and the caricature became increasingly blurred. He was often portrayed with the devil's horns, cloven hooves in place of feet, and a wickedly handsome visage in much the way Dracula had come to be portrayed in Hollywood.

Barnard had a multifaceted personality, both secretive and urbane, yet he was strikingly reflective about himself. He would often acknowledge the flaws in his personality and contemplate their origins. He was inclined to distance himself from people and was ceremonial in all respects, wearing only the most polished attire even when home alone. According to his wife, Helen, Barnard "thought that he was condemned to be maligned, betrayed, unfairly beleaguered, misjudged, underappreciated, and subjected to the trials of Hercules, but that by the use of his colossal resolve, determination, and assiduousness, he would eventually triumph."

Barnard was a shrewd, gifted man, but the most troubled of all the presidents. He assumed the worst in people and he brought out the worst in them. He adhered to the idea of being hardened. He believed it was this hardness that had brought him to the edge of greatness.

Barnard Christophe assumed that putting space between himself and other people was crucial for him as he advanced in his political profession and came to be president. Even with close friends, Christophe didn't believe in letting his hair down. He believed that one should keep one's difficulties to oneself.

His scandal-plagued presidency was only eclipsed by his ability to create division and an unprecedented class war within the United States. Divide and conquer was his motto, and he was able to enact it with brutal success. If people were too busy fighting one another, they had no time to realize what he really was and oust him from his position of power and self-indulgence. Those who disagreed with him were his enemies, and they were punished. President Christophe considered himself among the intellectually elite and often daydreamed of being a dictator. While espousing the views of wealth redistribution publically, in private he only embraced the redistribution of wealth and power from his acknowledged opponents to his supporters and friends. Political cronyism was the alpha-dog philosophy that ruled in Washington, DC.

Christophe was not a big fan of the fossil fuel industry; however, with so many in his party facing a close reelection, he had to make some move to show that he would help them. Christophe's friends and supporters belonged to those who promoted alternative energy, but big oil did have deep pockets. Making a show of helping and actually coming to their aid were two different things, which is why he waited for his chief of staff with growing impatience.

He viewed NED and CLU as an evil alliance on steroids, and his mind was always occupied with ways to destroy or minimize their activities whenever possible. He was convinced that NED worked secretly to undermine his power within the Beltway. He was aware that they were planning on triggering another coup in Venezuela due to both the pressure from big-oil interests and because Gomez was considered vulnerable. Christophe had no love for interfering with other governments. In fact, he believed that the United States' involvement in these affairs smacked of imperialism. Although there had been significant changes in foreign operations policy under the Whitehall administration in CLU, these changes would be quite controversial if only the public were aware of them. But CLU had more cloaking than a stealth bomber.

Despite the pushback from the current president and his lackeys, Koshka had been able to revert CLU back to its hard-line practices of bygone years. These practices, Koshka thought, were best left to those who needed to know about them. The AFL-CIO, union members, and John Q. Public didn't need to know. However, as president, Christophe did have some power. By working behind-the-scenes, he could sabotage any effort to topple the Venezuelan government by the American labor movement and the CIA.

He had no great love for either of those two institutions, though he feigned a special camaraderie with organized labor. In that way he was much like former President Jimmy Carter. Oh, how organized labor embraced the Georgia peanut farmer! All the while the man had done more damage to organized labor than any other president in history. Carter had help getting his antilabor agenda pushed through by none other than Ted Kennedy himself. The deregulation of the airlines—Carter. The plan to deregulate trucking—Carter (although President Reagan was the one to finish pushing that plan through.) The big one was the PATCO strike. That was when the air-traffic controllers went on a nationwide strike in 1981, practically paralyzing the country. While Reagan got all the credit, the real brains behind breaking the strike, and therefore the actual union, was President Jimmy Carter. It was his plan, as he expected to be reelected—and therefore he would be the president faced with the looming labor dispute. However, he was defeated, and it was Ronald Reagan who inherited the strike. Reagan, ever a practical man, saw no reason to reinvent the wheel and used the plan developed by Carter.

President Christophe sighed and wondered where his Ted Kennedy was. Why was he always forced to carry on by himself?

As he paced the Oval Office, his mind playing through different scenarios, his chief of staff was announced and ambled into the room.

"Peter, I wanted to talk with you about our little problem in South America," said Christophe. His white teeth, which normally were displayed in a charismatic smile for the public, were now clenched in a grimace.

Peter Abercrombie was as good a chief of staff as a president could hope for. Eager and willing, the middle-aged man showed an unswerving desire to not only please the president he served but also to shield him from anything that might harm his reputation. It was Peter who handled the undesirable chores. He never shared the how or who, allowing President Christophe plausible deniability.

"Mr. President." Peter bowed slightly, as was his habit.

"Peter, NED has sent Andy Wayne down there. This is quite a problem. Once again, the US's imperialism is imposing itself on a foreign government. CLU is working with the CIA to overthrow a progressive, nationalist government in a third-world country, just like the overthrow of Allende in Chile and

Arbenz in Guatemala!" the President exclaimed. "I'm afraid I'm handing off another burden to you."

"It's not much of a burden at all. Please don't worry yourself over it. You have so many crushing problems on your plate. This endeavor in South America is a standard move by CLU. It's what they were created to do. Destabilize a government here, launch a labor revolution there. Over the decades, they have gotten despicably good at it."

The president forced a smile. "You know, Peter, I don't believe it's in the US's best interest for CLU to be there. Unfortunately, CLU was set up so that it could not be directly controlled by either the president or Congress. This is a midterm election year, and I'll be forced to bear this on my shoulders should they fail. All fingers will be pointed directly at me. What would I say or do? This cannot be explained. I have no idea how to proceed right now. The Middle East is in turmoil, and now I have this situation thrust at me."

"Sir, please don't worry about this matter any further. Allow me to deal with it. I can handle this on my own."

As soon as Peter closed the door to the Oval Office behind him, he took out his personal secured sat phone and dialed a number to another secured phone that was deeply imbedded in his memory. It was a number he would never write down.

"Ah, Denise." Peter smiled as a woman's voice answered on the second ring. "You heard that there might be a problem in South America?"

"I did. What would you like me to do? Which side of this are we on?"

Peter ducked into an empty room, making sure that he could not be overheard.

"Go to Brazil and find Andy Wayne. Make sure he fails. Make sure he can't defend himself against the charges of failure in the future. People go missing all the time in the jungles of South America. Perhaps he'll like it there too much to leave. I don't know, but come up with something. This is your area of expertise."

Denise's lip curled with satisfaction. She liked running her own show. Occasionally she would have a client who would place certain conditions or restraints on her. Things like "Make it look like a random killing or an accident." Even Peter often added caveats. His particular favorite was to make it look like a suicide. For some reason that gave him perverse pleasure. Denise often wondered how much the president knew about his chief of staff's activities. She reasoned that he probably did not know anything, but she would bet her life that he certainly suspected something.

"And Denise? Give me CLU on a platter."

"I should get started," she replied. "You've given me a tall order, and I need to move quickly."

She was all business. Peter heard her break off the connection and was completely confident that she could fulfill the contract. It was not the first time he had used her special skills.

Denise Menon had worked for the CIA in a previous life. She now freelanced, and her favorite client was Peter Abercrombie. Her favorite adversary was Koshka—mostly because Koshka refused to subcontract work out to her. Koshka believed that it was easier to control these kinds of things if you kept them in-house. She viewed people like Denise as less than pure when it came to fighting for the "Cause." This attitude pissed Denise off. Koshka seemed to think she was better than Denise. Denise was a professional, however, and she only engaged in wet work (killing)or other operations when money was involved. Peter had been keeping her busy. Mostly with sabotage. The president had a long list of enemies.

Peter and Denise had much in common. Neither really believed in anything, because that would require trust. Both felt that it required sacrifice and brutal strength on their part to destroy their enemies before their enemies could destroy them.

Peter had indulged in sex with Denise on two occasions, but it never progressed to a more stable affair. Both carried their self-serving intent into the bedroom, which left any sexual relations strangely unfulfilling for either party. Even sex for just the pure physical pleasure required a give-and-take, but neither of them was capable of giving, which doomed any long-term entanglements from forming.

Five

The inability to connect was not a problem that Andy Wayne and Joyia Gabriella had to contend with. A soft tap at Andy's door, the door quickly opens, a beautiful woman greets a handsome man, clothes are quickly shed, and this is followed by a lengthy, raucous lovemaking session. Which brings both to the point they were at now: lying in bed, completely satiated, studying the Venezuelan file, and sharing strategy.

Joyia's family had a long, storied history with espionage in Latin America. The Gabriella family was as intertwined with the politics that shaped South America, as was Simon Bolivar. After World War II, with Europe firmly under the influences of Jay Lovestone and Irving Brown, the United States and the CIA focused their attention on South America. Democracy, like any other government ideology, yearns to spread its likeness to other borders. It is just more benign in its mission. Its main competitor was communism in a post-World War II world. The USSR and the USA fought for world dominance. Needing a pro-American activist to operate in Latin America, the CIA turned to its favorite recruiter, David Dubinsky, the same man who brought Jay Lovestone and, by proxy, Irving

Brown to the table. Dubinsky did not disappoint. This time he brought in an émigré from what had been fascist Italy—Serafino Romualdi. It was through the efforts of Serafino that the Federation of Trade Unions Council (FTUC), a forerunner of CLU, became active in Latin America.

At the time of Serafino's arrival in South America, the Latin American Confederation of Labor (CTAL) was the prevailing labor organization in Latin America after World War II. The political orientation of the CTAL was leftist, leaning well into communist party affiliation. Like his most effective counterparts in Europe, Romualdi's strategy to break the back of CTAL's political power was to create an alternative anticommunist labor organization. As in the past, the CIA and the US State Department stood in the wings, waiting to lend a hand to assist the efforts of America's labor union.

It was difficult to win affiliation status with the pro-democracy trade unions of the United States. Normally, it required a nod from the State Department. This was becoming more difficult to get as more and more communist sympathizers found their way into government positions within the State Department. Romualdi was no trembling flower, and he launched a vicious attack on the State Department. Romualdi stated regarding the State Department policymakers, "If not openly allied, they are definitely supporting groups in Latin America who are enemies of the American way of life and who are followers of the Communist Party line." His verbal assault hit the mark, and the State Department was quick to aid FTUC in South America.

No sooner did Serafino get the blessing of the State Department than he received the backing of industrial titans such as Nelson Rockefeller. The doors then swung open for Romualdi's welcome into every state-sanctioned "free" trade-union office in Latin America. Through one or more of these already established free trade-union offices, Romualdi would launch his counterrevolution to the CTAL.

Not long after Romualdi's success in Washington, DC, the Inter-American Confederation of Labor made its appearance. The CIT, as it was called, was created by the merging of the free trade-union organizations already established in seventeen Latin American countries. The merging of these smaller organizations finally gave muscle to a CTAL alternative, and a dual union wedge had effectively been driven home by 1948.

The CIT lasted almost two years, when changing relations between AFL and CIO allowed for a bolder and broader approach in Latin America. And that approach Romaldi accomplished with the valuable help of Joyia's grandfather. It was this family tradition that first got her involved with CUT in Brazil. Her family had benefited financially over the decades from its alliance with America's covert organizations, but it had also suffered losses. Her father died during the effort to overthrow Chavez. His death had propelled Joyia to the position she was in today.

Andy glanced at the file he had on the current Venezuelan president. "Tell me about Venezuela and Gomez."

"This Gomez is having a hard time in his first year in power. Venezuela's economy is the worst-performing in Latin

America this year, a problem exacerbated by a drop in oil output, power outages, and soaring inflation," Joyia said. "I think it'd be easy to stir up the old embers of *revolución*."

"Perhaps, but do we know where those old embers are still smoldering?" he asked.

"Oh, *mi amante*." She addressed him as her lover, as she did with all her dalliances. "I never lose touch with those who need me the most. Besides our old friends, we have many university students who are always ready to protest or rally against the establishment. We just have to encourage them in their view of being able to change the world."

"I think we need to meet up with our friends of old," said Andy. "As for the students, perhaps it's time that they really do change the world—at least the current one in Venezuela."

"And I have read your mind before you knew to think such thoughts. I have already arranged for us to meet. But it must be in the mountains by the border. They cannot risk going back and forth across the border. The *cabrón* who runs that country watches, for he is not as safe as he wants to be. They would raise suspicion. The Chavez coup is not so far from his memory."

Andy cursed. He hated the idea of leaving civilization or exerting himself. He much preferred clandestine meetings in homes or dark-lit bars. He had met others in CLU who thrived on the excitement of "roughing it" or facing physical confrontation. Not Andy. He was a man who enjoyed the thrill of planning strategy in a well-appointed bar while others carried out the actual killing and dying parts. In fact, he liked to see the fruits of his labor on CNN or Fox News while relaxing at home, whichever his mood dictated he watch that night. They should have just shot Chavez all those years ago as he had encouraged them to do. Then they would not be sitting here today. Chavez would not have been alive to return to power; the back of his support would have been broken, and there would not have been Gomez there to succeed him. In that way Andy always agreed with Koshka. Never leave them alive. That is why Gaddafi was killed, and so was Hussein. The others who lived only did so because they had friends on the Board and were promised sanctuary in other countries, where they could live out the remainder of their lives in lavish comfort. Koshka was a firm believer in the scorched-earth method when it came to deposing an unfriendly. And in this area, Andy completely agreed with her.

The Center for Labor Unity was once again in South America, this time in Venezuela, just as it was in Chile in 1973. Its operations in Venezuela were being funded by the US government, and once again the money funding the expedition was being supplied through the shadow organization, the Democracy Endowment Movement, which would always remain hidden from union members and the American public.

As with all its operations, the efforts of Andy Wayne and the CLU were being used to support the efforts of reactionary labor and business leaders, helping to destabilize a government that had made every effort to hamper the efforts of the United States and her allies to form that one-world government, with the United States being the flagship under which all others would be absorbed.

Contrary to popular belief, countries like Venezuela were not fighting for independence. They were fighting for the alternative. There was no misspeak on Bush the younger's part when he referred to the Axis of Evil. Indeed, there were two teams, so to speak, trying to form their version of the perfect world. On the one side were the United States and her allies. Faced with pushback from their own citizenry, this faction has made several attempts at unification. The Eurozone was a step toward that one-world government. However, it has been tripped up by each country attempting to remain sovereign while also reaching for the holy grail of a one-world order. Countries such as Greece were not as frugal with their finances as places such as Germany, and the Greeks bristled at outside interference as their country entered into a financial meltdown, and that was affecting other members of the Eurozone. Such was the nature of countries. They wanted to maintain their sovereignty and fought against relinquishing control; and it was that very nature that those promoting world governance fought against.

The other faction enveloped Iran, Venezuela, Bolivia, North Korea, and Palestine, which received support from Hezbollah, Al-Qaeda, and the Muslim Brotherhood. That team played by no rules and made the oddest of partnerships. While the US-led conglomerate was secular in its composition, the Iranian-led faction was a discombobulated mess of extreme Muslim groups, Communist/atheist countries, and a large Christian population based in South America.

The CLU in itself could not be viewed as completely good or completely bad. The means to an end generally involved a major effort to alleviate poverty and carry out significant land reform in both urban and rural areas, as it strove to change political institutions that had long worked to marginalize those at the lowest rungs in society.

But ultimately it was all about power and control. Providing or enabling a government-dependent lifestyle also led to a more controlled society: control of speech, control of income, control of health care, and eventually control of thought. The United States was more successful at delivering a mechanism of mass population control than any other country. Through the illusion of a two-party system that truly did experience strife among the political ruling class, the citizens of the United States felt they still had freedom and control over their government.

The Democrats and Republicans were working toward the same goal; it was the process of getting there that was often in dispute. Countries like North Korea looked at the success of the United States and wanted to destroy all that it had accomplished, loath to admit the United States and her allies were way ahead in the world-domination game. This is understandable when viewed from the perspective of a petty dictator who starves his own people to feed his war machine and megalomaniac psychosis. And like Venezuela's government under President Hugo Chavez, Venezuela's new president, Manuel Gomez, had opposed a number of actions by the US government, this time by the Christophe administration.

Venezuelan President Manuel Gomez, a former midlevel army officer, was proud of his indigenous roots and had an avid interest in addressing the exclusion of those on the lowest rungs of society. Following Chavez's release from prison, Gomez helped create a movement. An important part of the movement's popularity with the poor stemmed from the belief that "the plight of the poor took priority over the protection of private property."

Gomez and his efforts were contradictory: although he promoted the idea of including the poor in governmental procedure, he has done so in a top-down manner. His movement was ideologically blurred and internally contradictory. It was not dedicated to constructing organizations to empower the underprivileged. That was because at the heart of all petty dictators was the desire to remain in power; and most believed that if you empowered others, eventually your own power would be challenged.

Although despots like Gomez claimed to have been democratically elected, the facts presented by international observers challenged this assertion. Locking up your opponent does not lend itself to a fair voting process. However, back to the poor. The have-nots in Venezuela outnumbered the haves, which is why, as a strategy, playing to the reallocation of private wealth was quite popular. The same strategy was playing itself out in the United States, but the confiscation of money from those not within the power circle was done in small increments, thereby avoiding any serious outcry. Consequently, in Venezuela, as in the United States, money had been redistributed, along with the power, only not to the poor. In Venezuela, it had been redistributed by Chavez to his supporters. Gomez saw his own personal fortunes improve dramatically.

Surprisingly, though, the plight of the poor remained the same. The only thing that changed was the future of the middle class, which only dwindled. The opportunity that once existed for the youth who were graduating from high schools and universities vanished, replaced by empty shelves in the grocery stores, where even the most basic and mundane necessities such as toilet paper disappeared. The youth of Venezuela seethed with unrest and waited restlessly for the "dogs of war" to be unleashed. The caldron of discontent only needed the finesse of an expert in revolutions to turn up the heat until it boiled over.

Just the sort of job that Andy Wayne relished.

In 2002, the AFL-CIO's international arm—CLU—was greatly embarrassed when it came to light that it had been supporting actors in Venezuela who participated in the short-lived coup against President Hugo Chavez. Whereas in the past years, the poor had reacted in a positive way to this class warfare message of wealth redistribution, recently they seemed to have become jaded by the same message being hawked by Gomez.

In public, those who resided in the squalor of the slums in the hills above Caracas spoke little, but behind closed doors, far from the ears and eyes of the *federales*, the whispered words of revolt were echoed from home to home. A married couple who had supported Chavez and raised their sons to revere the revolutionary leader now questioned what seemed to be misplaced loyalty. Both husband and wife had worked for the government for years, yet they still were unable to raise their family out of the slums they started in decades ago. Perhaps this had not been the way after all. A tension hung over Venezuela's capital like an ever-pressing weight. Even though the sun cast its brilliant light over Caracas, darkness pervaded the air. Caracas waited for Andy and his match to light the fuse.

Andy's work was made much easier by the fact that the United States and her allies had pumped over $30 million into cultivating the youth of Venezuela. Through facades of student organizations, pro-family groups, and educational neighborhood outreach, the United States had indoctrinated millions of young passionate Venezuelans about what they should be entitled to.

As the saying goes, the truth can hurt. And the truth was that even after Chavez returned to power in 2002, social conflict continued just beneath the calm surface. Venezuelan society remained turbulent. Shortly after Chavez returned to power, there was a sixty-three-day strike, led by senior management in Venezuela's oil industry. This strike produced acts of sabotage and rewarded the saboteurs with a cataclysmic 27 percent drop in the gross domestic product in the early part of 2003, causing great public and financial mayhem and divesting the government of colossal amounts of cash that it had been using to prop up social agendas.

The battle against *Chavismo* (the socialist form of government created by Chavez) had continued ever since, with the US-based CLU intensely committed to the struggle being waged there.

NED had long been active across South America. In Venezuela alone, it had had its hand in political affairs since the early 1990s. Some believed it was for the oil—after all, Venezuela was the fifth-largest oil producer in the world. According to explanations collected from NED itself, NED provided over $35 million to Venezuelan and American organizations working in Venezuela between 2002 and 2013. Of that amount, 61 percent was awarded to CLU for its work with the CTV. In December 2014, NED pumped another $1,099,352 into various groups in Venezuela, of which CLU got $116,001 for its work with CTV.

The AFL-CIO gave a different accounting to the public, in case any of them should care. The assistant director of the AFL-CIO's International Affairs department, while exalting the labor organization's work abroad, wrote in the spring 2014 issue of *New Labor Network*, "[O]ur entire esprit de corps program with the CTV totaled less than $10,000 in funding of the Confederation's exceedingly positive in-house democratization method…"

Now Andy was working with the CTV, utilizing assets from the Workers Telecommunications Union (a US-based union) where the lovely Joyia Gabriella was employed, and would be meeting with students, young professionals, and others with a rebellious bent to stoke the fires of unrest even more. After all, labor unions held the monopoly on agitating, whether it was within a workforce or a community. Andy was just supersizing the effort. As June approached, CTV, WTU and another coconspirator, FEDECAMARAS, the nation's business association, planned large-scale general strikes and lockouts of a size and violence level that would reach such a heated climax that it would eventually topple the Venezuelan government. A spectacular coup tantalized the mind and senses of Andy Wayne.

Andy and Joyia met with FEDECARAMAS representative Marco Ortega and Venezuelan union leader Francisco Morales three days after Andy's arrival in Brazil. Both Marco and Francisco were in Brazil for a South American trade conference, and it was easy for them to route their return to Venezuela through Boa Vista. This brought great relief to Andy, who did not want the first meeting to be in the middle of nowhere with not even a glass of decent wine to sip while discussing the coming events. Instead, they would be able to meet at a comfortable, family-owned restaurant just down the street from his hotel.

Marco Ortega arrived first. His greeting was jovial and effusive as he slapped Andy on the back and gave Joyia an appreciative look combined with a hearty hug. Marco was a burly man whose bald pate had a small fringe of salt-and-pepper hair that circled his head just above his ears, accenting the lack of hair on top. Marco was married and had eight children. And although he was a man and enjoyed the view Joyia presented to his eyes, he was also a devout Catholic who deeply loved his family. Marco's wife came from a good family heavily involved in the Catholic Church and considered a part of the upper middle class. Just as Marco ordered a Caipirinha, a traditional Brazilian drink prepared with a Brazilian liquor called cachaça, Francisco joined the group at the table. No two men could be as opposite as the two Venezuelans. Francisco was a string bean of a man with more hair then he knew how to style properly. He finally capitulated to its willful and wild ways and settled for capturing it into a ponytail. Whereas Marco's eyes shone honest admiration for a beautiful woman when he looked at Joyia, Francisco's eyes showed nothing. Francisco played for the other team.

Whereas Marco was jovial and hearty, Francisco was quiet and reserved. However, inside the head of the gay Latino was the brain of an exquisite strategist. Needless to say, Francisco had neither the religious fervor that dominated Marco's life nor many of the conservative values that influenced Marco's beliefs, but what he did share with Marco was a deep hatred for Chavismo and the current government in Venezuela. Both men believed in democracy, capitalism, and freedom—luxuries not easily found in Venezuela currently.

After greetings were exchanged and Francisco ordered himself a Brazilian beer called Skol, the group got down to quietly discussing their plans.

Marco offered FEDECARAMAS as the lead organization in public protests, which Andy quickly shot down.

"It's not that FEDERCARAMAS is not a capable organization in doing this, but it would not play well with the press—or the world, for that matter. No, the best place for FEDERCARAMAS in this is to be able to help in monetary support and to offer support in the area of material things and safe houses if need be." Andy paused. "At least at first."

Francisco jumped in at that point. "You want the workers to lead this?"

Andy smiled. "Of course. I am with organized labor. No offense, Marco. Businesses don't revolt; workers do. The world always bleeds for the workers. This is how I see this unrolling. First Francisco will get the workers organized for strikes across the country. Then we need to get the students involved as well as anyone with celebrity status in Venezuela. We need student marches as well as celebrities coming out and standing with the students and workers. Watch some tapes on Occupy Wall Street, and I have some video from Tunisia, which may help as well. Although their whole thing there was somewhat different because of the Muslim aspect. However, if you find any volunteers for self-immolation, don't talk them out of it. For some reason the world press is captivated by people who set themselves on fire for a cause. It's good press. Only after all these events take place does FEDERCARAMAS step in. Marco, release a press statement, something to the effect that the businesses of Venezuela sympathize with the marchers. It is the desire of business in Venezuela to lift their countrymen out of poverty, but the government's stranglehold through laws and regulation make it impossible for this to happen. Businesses want Venezuelans to be able to have money to buy a lot of their products, but unfortunately the government has erected too many barriers that keep people in poverty. Any attempt to fight this, and a business owner risks President Gomez seizing his business."

"Did you just do that little speech now, how you say, um, off the top of your head?" Joyia asked.

Andy nodded. "Something like that could work, especially if the business owners start joining the marchers, CEOs, etcetera."

"That's good. *Muy bueno*. You are truly an artiste of *revolución*," Joyia declared while patting his arm.

Marco's head bobbed up and down enthusiastically. "Si, we can do that. The business community is ready, but we were ready in 2002 when we tried to get rid of Chavez. That did not go so well." Marco's mouth formed a pout as he pulled at his lower lip. "My people may need encouragement to go down this path again."

Andy excelled at his craft, and he felt that his mastery as a community organizer was due in whole to being a devout disciple of Saul Alinsky's "Rules for Radicals." And Andy knew the twelve most important rules by heart. Tonight was about Rule 1: "Power is not only what you have but what the enemy thinks you have." And power was derived from two main sources—money and people.

"They will need nothing but to see the working people and the students in the streets," Francisco said softly. "Strikes that paralyze the country, government buildings set on fire..." His voice trailed off. He turned to Andy. His eyes were very serious. "This black bloc that they were doing in your country, I want to do that here."

Black bloc is a tactic used in protests where people wear black clothing, sunglasses, ski masks, motorcycle helmets with padding, or other face-concealing articles of clothing. The clothing is used to conceal marchers' identities and hinder criminal prosecution by making it difficult to distinguish between participants. It is also used to protect their faces and eyes from pepper spray, which law enforcement often uses to daze protestors. The tactic allows the activists to appear as one large, unified mass and promotes solidarity.

"Of course. In fact, I think that if we outfit our rebellion in the style exhibited by the OWS and the ninety-nine percent marchers, we will actually motivate sympathy rallies and strikes in other areas of the world."

"The FEDERCARAMAS would be happy to supply masks and black clothing for the protesters. As well as any other funding that will be needed," Marco quickly promised.

Francisco nodded. "This is good, as many would not be able to afford such things."

"Marco," Andy interjected. "I will set you up with some suppliers in the US. We can bring it in through Brazil and Colombia, circumventing customs in Venezuela."

Marco nodded. "This would be good."

The borders between the countries were porous, particularly the border Venezuela shared with Colombia, which saw more than its fair share of smuggling and contraband flow both ways.

"Marco, where you could help a lot is through your Catholic connections. We need to mobilize the poor, the farmers, etcetera. The high population of devout Catholics in the country would be open to encouragement in that direction from the church."

The discussion continued back and forth for several more hours. The plan would be for the CTV to lead the work stoppages and strikes that would galvanize an already angry population.

In the end they all agreed that Andy's plan would work, but it had to be implemented in stages until it caught fire, sending the whole country into chaos. Both Marco and Francisco adapted parts of the plan to work with their organizations.

Francisco would have by far the hardest job at the start. Although the fuel for rebellion was already present in the population, lighting it would be tricky. A large enough group would have to take to the streets at one time from various smaller groups. Too small a group and they would be crushed before they could get started. And getting crushed would scare others away from doing the same thing. And although Francisco was a master at instigation, this was instigation on a larger scale than he had ever dealt with before. However, he felt fairly confident he could pull it off.

Joyia signaled the waiter over and ordered chimarrão, a special tea that is generally shared with groups of friends. The tea was passed around in a metal cup, as was the tradition, and everyone took turns drinking from it. The activity seemed to instill camaraderie and a sealing of the deal, so to speak. They were now all in this together.

Andy's destabilization efforts in Venezuela would not be a narrow effort, utilizing only labor organizations. That would be only one component of a multiple-pronged attack that included supporting as well as uniting special-interest groups: a peasant organization that opposed land-grabbing government reform; an educational organization that suggested massive education reforms; an organization seeking to incite a military rebellion; a civic association that had worked to mobilize middle-class neighborhoods to "defend themselves" from high taxes and confiscations; a civil justice group that opposed the Gomez government because they saw it as a lawless group of thugs; a "leadership group" that supported restructuring the metropolitan Caracas police, whose behavior had become markedly more repressive over the past year; and a number of other anti-Gomez organizations, each of which had coincidently received funding from NED recently.

Back home, John Q. Public was blissfully unaware, as were the union members whose dues contributed, even if on a small level, to CLU's activities. If the American press was somehow motivated by rumors swirling on the conspiracy blogs to investigate CLU's activities, they would start by visiting CLU's website. If they were so motivated, they would have then clicked on the "Where We Work" link. They would then notice that Venezuela was notably absent from the list of countries where the CLU did business. Similarly, the CLU mentioned nothing about Venezuela in its most recent annual report. However, if that reporter was not easily put off and then went to the website of one of the CLU's biggest patrons, the NED, that reporter would find something quite different. In a section entitled "Latin America Regional," NED explained that it had recently given enormous funding to the CLU to carry out work both in Colombia and Venezuela.

That reporter might also note that this amount was in addition to another $2 million the NED—which, on its website, openly expressed contempt for "Twenty-First-Century Socialism"—gave to the CLU for other Latin American work.

And, as the NED explained, "in Venezuela, CLU will build on its ongoing work with partners…" Quite portentous words, given the nature of the work and partners the CLU had up to this point been involved with in Venezuela. However, luckily for NED and CLU, no American journalist was motivated to look into the matter.

But there were three questions that Andy Wayne and CLU would need to answer for the PR spin machine that would have to bring the sympathy of the world to the side of their Venezuelan revolutionaries.

First, how did these efforts to overthrow a tyrant help meet the needs and aspirations of the poorest 80 percent of the population?

Second, how did working to destabilize the elected government of Venezuela help workers and their families in the United States? After all, the support of the American people would be needed to support the fledgling revolution with weaponry and the resulting government materially. This one he felt he could answer simply enough. He would give protesters small American flags to wave, and at every opportunity, he would find a way to showcase people singing the United States' praises to any reporter who had a camera crew. Americans were suckers for people who longed to imitate them as much as they were suckers for underdogs.

And third, how would they keep the Russians from getting involved? Russia was much more of a loose cannon than China. Russia was always and only on Russia's side, whereas China understood how the American need for the cheap material items they produced fueled their growing economy—an economy that would fail if the United States could no longer feed the belly of the Chinese beast. Russia was not so practical; its leadership was still trying to resurrect the powerhouse of the old Soviet Union. Fortunately for Russia, the United States was making it easy.

Andy's plan did involve some of the same mechanics from the plan used when CLU and the CIA attempted to overthrow Chavez by bringing the CTV together with FEDERCARAMAS. This time there would hopefully be a positive twist in the ending. Previously, CLU had moved its office (which was in charge of the entire Andean region) from Caracas, Venezuela, to Rio de Janeiro, Brazil, just three weeks before the Chavez coup took place, and they never attempted to move the office back when the coup failed. Of course, Chavez banned them from operating in his country, so that probably made the decision to stay in Rio easier. This time the plan would be to reopen the offices in Caracas after Gomez was removed from power.

It was not publicly known that the CLU—which received nearly all of its funding from federal grants ($28 million out of its total annual budget of $30 million)—was currently in Venezuela. However, whispers had started to float through the hallways of the Venezuelan embassy in DC that the CIA was back in Venezuela and plotting to unseat President Gomez.

Six

The evening was a pleasant one as Andy and Joyia left the restaurant and headed back to the hotel. A light breeze teased the leaves of the tropical plants, bringing Boa Vista some relief from the humidity.

The two walked in silence, and neither noticed the figure watching them from the park, protected by the dense foliage as well as the shadows of the night that were quickly descending.

Denise watched the pair make their way nonchalantly toward the hotel, confident of their safety. And for tonight they could be. Denise would not be taking a shot at Andy this evening in the quiet streets of Boa Vista. She had only arrived that morning and still felt a little weary from the long trip. She needed a plan. Nothing too complex. Denise embraced simplicity. The less that could go wrong, the better. She also wanted to make sure that her escape was assured. The last place she wanted to spend her life was in a South American prison.

Before leaving the United States, Denise had made a quick call to Servicio Bolivariano de Inteligencia (SEBIN), Venezuela's equivalent of the CIA. Back in the early days of her freelance career, Denise had done a couple of odd jobs for them in Peru and Colombia. Venezuela was not always on good terms with its neighbors and, on a couple of occasions, had offered asylum to enemies of each of those countries. Denise had carried out her contracts with them with extraordinary efficiency and had earned the divisional agent in charge, the man who had hired her, a promotion.

Denise now had information for the man to put him in her debt as well as advance his career once more. This friendly heads-up guaranteed Denise a smooth passage if she should be taken into custody after her contract on Andy was fulfilled. She had no intentions of being spotted, let alone caught; but plans can go bad, and it was always worthwhile to have a safety net. It was not often she had one when she went to work.

Denise sat down on a bench in the park and waited ten minutes, giving the pair a good head start into the hotel, and then made her way to the same destination. Denise had a room in the same hotel. Neither Andy nor Joyia knew what she looked like, so that gave her an advantage. By getting a room in the same hotel, she would have a vantage point from which to track the comings and goings of Andy as well as others who made contact with him. Denise checked her watch and headed out of the park.

Andy and Joyia were seated at the bar in the hotel when Denise arrived. Andy looked up at her and then away. There was nothing distinguishable about the woman. She was certainly not a woman whom Andy would notice on any level. Denise was average: average height, average build, and average flat brown hair. Her eyes were hazel; her clothes were something a tourist might wear. She was plain—the kind of person who didn't register in anyone's memory. She blended in and therefore possessed the perfect physical characteristics for someone in her profession. Denise ordered a Skol and sipped it as she watched the two activists in the reflection of the mirror that decorated the wall beside her table.

The pair huddled with their heads close together, and it was obvious to even the most casual observer that there was a sexual connection. Joyia's eyes began to sparkle in direct correlation with the alcohol she was consuming, and Andy was encouraging her to have another glass. Both toasted each other with a shot glass filled with tequila. Joyia slung her arm around Andy's neck and whispered something in his ear that earned her a playful kiss from Andy. The bartender lined up another set of shots. Denise sipped her beer again, although by this time it had gotten warm. She considered the fact that the man she was hired to kill was an incompetent drunk. He certainly was no professional. That should make things easy for her, but at the same time, it was deflating to think that her talents were wasted on a guy who could just as easily be killed by a hired thug.

She concluded that the only person who would be approaching the pair would be the bartender. Their revolutionary activities were over for the evening. Denise rose from her table and threw down a couple of Brazil's reals, the equivalent of about thirty-seven cents in US money. She didn't want to tip too much or too little.

Denise headed up to her room. Although she was somewhat relaxed, having found the environment around her to be free of any threats, her eyes were constantly looking for some proof that the situation had changed.

At the door to her room, she found the thin strand of hair she had attached to the door handle with a light spritz of hairspray still in place. Had someone opened the door, that hair would not still be there. Once in her room, she went directly to the window overlooking the street in front of the hotel. She not only chose this view, she insisted on it. It would be highly unlikely for someone to scale the front of the building on a main street or rappel down from the roof and attempt to get in her room without being seen. All this compulsive attention to detail made her the success she had become at this kind of wet work.

On her bed were three boxes sent to her by SEBIN. A courier had delivered them shortly after she checked into the hotel. The largest box held an HK PSG1, a German-made sniper rifle. It had an eight-hundred-meter range and came with a twenty-round detachable magazine. Denise would not need twenty rounds unless something went horribly wrong.

In the next box was a Judge, made by the Brazilian company Taurus. The Judge was a five-shot revolver designed to chamber either .410 bore shot shells or a .45 Colt cartridge. It was good for close range.

In the third box was a basic 9 mm Ruger. They had made sure she would not lack for firepower. Earlier that day Denise had gone out shopping and purchased a hiking backpack, some dehydrated food, and a hollow-handled survival knife. Denise did not know if Andy would be hiking across the border, but she thought she should be prepared. Crossing the border into

Venezuela was not for the faint of heart. It was a dangerous journey where the hiker would be exposed to robbery or assault.

Denise went over each weapon carefully to make sure each was clean and operational. When she was satisfied with the condition of her tools of the trade, she put them away in the backpack, having carefully broken down and wrapped the sniper rifle. It was, after all, the most valuable and most likely weapon of choice in this scenario.

With everything neatly organized and ready to go, Denise picked up her sat phone and placed a call to Peter.

"I hope you had a pleasant flight," Peter answered.

"It was no more or no less pleasant than any other flight," Denise responded.

"Is the hotel to your liking?" Peter asked.

"Peter, this is a secure line," Denise admonished.

"Yes, but you don't know who might be listening in on my end," he retorted.

"Well, then, get somewhere that we don't have to worry about that. I hate this little game of read-between-the-lines."

"Well, then, please tell me all."

"He's here at the hotel with the little tramp from Brazil. They met with two men. I didn't recognize them, but I've e-mailed pictures to you. I also sent the pictures to my contacts in Venezuela. I need to know who they are. Tonight he was in the bar, drinking like a pig, so I don't think he's planning an early start in the morning."

"I'll see what I can do on the names of the men," Peter replied. "How soon can you remove him?"

"Soon. I'm waiting to see how he plans on getting into Venezuela. I'll call you if I have anything else."

She hung up without waiting for a reply. She changed into some workout clothes that were comfortable to sleep in but also good for a quick escape, if necessary. She slipped off into a light slumber with the 9 mm on the nightstand by the bed.

Andy and Joyia were not encumbered with any paranoia or fear as they made their way to Andy's room on the same floor as Denise. Once inside, they both attempted to undress each other at the same time. The door to the room slammed shut as they fell to the floor, both getting tangled in the clothes that fell around their feet.

Across the hall, Denise heard the ruckus and realized that she could rest easy. Nothing that she needed to be concerned about would be happening tonight.

Seven

The morning sun shone brightly into Andy's hotel room. Outside the window, some hotel guests were already making themselves comfortable on the lounges distributed around the pool. Andy was trimming his beard as Joyia showered.

"What time do we meet these Americans from your State Department?" Joyia called out from the shower.

"In about an hour and a half, so no dilly-dallying," Andy responded.

"What's this dilly and dally you speak of? I have no dillies or dallies," Joyia said as she stepped out of the shower and dried off.

Andy didn't even spare a glance in her direction. Today was all business. And despite Denise's first impression of him, Andy was an extremely competent agent provocateur. He was a well-seasoned soldier in the war on renegade governments. He had not survived this long without having ample skill. The last twenty-four hours were business and fun; from here on out, it would be all business. He dressed comfortably in a loose cotton shirt and a comfortable pair of button-fly Levi's. Joyia dressed in a cotton maxi dress with a pair of flat sandals. Andy wore gym shoes—you never knew when you might have to run. That was Andy's motto. He had had to do a lot of running over the years.

Joyia tugged at her dress and turned to ask him where they were going.

"Trigos. I always enjoyed the brunch there, and the pastries aren't too shabby, either."

Andy preferred to have his meetings in public, and he preferred to decide on the public location at the last minute. It was harder to place eavesdropping devices that way. In a hotel room, someone with the right technology could listen through the wall. Phones were out because he liked to see all the players' reactions and reinforce the team spirit. Also, depending on the chatter level in a restaurant, outside listening devices would have a hard time picking out their voices among the many. Noisy people had their benefits.

Joyia nodded as she concentrated on putting her earrings on. She didn't need to ask who the people from the State Department would be, because she knew he wouldn't answer and that she would find out when they arrived at the restaurant.

Denise was awakened by the sound of the hotel door across the hallway from hers opening and Joyia's voice floating through the walls. *Shit, shit, shit,* Denise thought. This was why she slept in workout clothes. She had guessed wrong about his schedule. She would make a note to herself not to make that mistake again. Andy apparently was an early riser regardless of how late his night lasted.

She scrambled to get her shoes on, grabbed her bag, and rushed out the door. Not wanting to wait for the elevator, she ran down the stairs. Once into the hotel lobby, she gathered her composure and walked out the doors—again, with few noticing her. Once outside she looked both right and left without spotting them at first. But after a second look, she saw Joyia's straw sun hat across the street, heading north. Denise quickly fell in behind them at a distance.

The red brick storefront of the restaurant was like millions of others scattered around the world in strip malls: large glass windows in front, and down the center of the eatery, a long, barlike table that allowed strangers to sit next to each other while they ate.

Andy led Joyia through the door. They were early, but Andy still looked to see if the State Department folks had beaten them to breakfast. They hadn't. Joyia and Andy decided on buffet and went to choose their food from a rather abundant selection. They bypassed the tables and seated themselves at the bar. As the bar enabled people to sit across from one another, Andy chose the second seat from the end on one side, and Joyia selected the third seat in on the other side. This left three seats for their guests. The place was moderately busy, but not so crowded that empty seats were hard to find. Both had hearty appetites after so much activity the night before, and neither felt any reason to wait for the others before they stated eating.

Denise did not want to risk entering the restaurant without some type of disguise. After Andy had glanced in her direction in the bar last night, he may have already forgotten her, but then again maybe he was more observant than she gave him credit for. Either way it wouldn't hurt to camouflage her appearance a bit. Denise looked around and spotted a tourist shop a few doors down from the restaurant and went in. A poncho woven by local artisans, a baseball cap with the word "Amazon" emblazoned across it, and some sunglasses were all she would need.

After tearing off price tags and throwing away the bag the store clerk had put her purchases in, Denise headed back to the restaurant. She entered right behind three other people. Andy glanced up sharply, and Denise felt a split second of panic, but it was the three people who entered before her that had caught his attention.

Denise brushed past them and made her way to a lone table. She ordered coffee and a pastry from a waitress and then settled in to view what was happening. She fished into her bag and dug out her cell phone. Pretending to be texting, Denise took photos of the two people sitting next to Joyia. The third person had his back to her, and she would have to wait for an opportunity to take his picture. The opportunity presented itself quickly when all three new arrivals got up and approached the buffet line. Denise looked at the pictures she had taken and felt they were good enough for someone to ID them.

The three people sat down once again with Joyia and Andy, this time with plates of food. Andy opened up the conversation by introducing the three newcomers to Joyia.

"All three are attached to the US embassy in Caracas. This is Dahlia. She is on her first assignment with the State Department, and she's a part of the agricultural attaché." Andy pointed to the man next to him. "Roland is a senior oil and energy analyst. He's the one who assists American oil companies in their business dealing in Venezuela."

Andy paused for a moment as he took a bite of a pastry. "And lastly is this jovial guy, Austin. Austin is here on temporary assignment with the embassy in order to promote education in Venezuela. And this," Andy said, using his thumb to point at her, "is Joyia. She's the Brazilian liaison between CUT and CLU."

With introductions out of the way, Andy opened the computer bag next to him and withdrew a sheaf of paper that had been captured in a binder.

"This, my friends," he said, holding up the binder, "is the plan."

The group leaned forward together. Andy flipped open the cover.

"Aren't you worried about putting this into writing?" Dahlia asked.

"No. I'd be more worried to put this on my computer or in an e-mail. No one looks for paper anymore. Plus, finding a plan on paper requires more effort than sitting at a desk hacking into accounts. In my mind you're more exposed on a computer." Andy felt that some technology was certainly a great thing in his line of work, but depending on it too much left you open to an attack by some unknown halfway around the world. Andy was familiar with that sector, having used it often against the governments he planned to unseat. "You will also notice no names, no incriminating marks, etcetera. It burns quite well also. In a computer you can never be sure if what you erase is completely gone."

Dahlia accepted Andy's logic, although her expression showed she had her doubts. Andy didn't bother to convince her. He didn't care what some college kid newbie at the State Department thought. They came out of college thinking they were smarter than the average person, yet they had no concept of what the real world encompassed. The professors gave them an idealized view that might work on paper but had little to do with reality.

Andy looked around the restaurant, which by now had pretty much emptied out. Even people in Boa Vista had jobs to get to. On the one hand, it spared them from anyone sitting too close; on the other hand, it didn't have the cacophony of voices that Andy preferred to clutter the airwaves. As he scanned the room, his eyes came to rest on a person sitting at a table alone. She was dressed as a tourist, with an Amazon baseball cap on and a poncho that made her shapeless. Underneath the bill of the ball cap, her eyes were completely focused on her cell phone, as she was engrossed in texting a rather lengthy message.

Something bothered Andy about her, but he couldn't put his finger on it. He looked at her again but still could not identify what it was about her that bothered him. She gave the impression of being completely oblivious to her surroundings. Andy gave his head a shake and got down to business. Paranoia in this line of work was healthy.

He carefully went over the outline of the plan. "First step: make sure that this has all the earmarks of an independent and spontaneous protest. We need to use the university and college students when we are able. They draw the most sympathy from the press, and in general, it doesn't take much to get them to fight for a cause bigger than themselves. Any parties that have been outspoken about their distaste for the current regime would have to absent themselves from the scene. At least on the surface. Any sign that an organized opposition party was involved takes away the sympathy for the students and common folk in the eyes of the rest of the world. For some reason it then becomes a clash of political parties, and in the current world, a clash of political parties is not cool enough to get any support from the celebrity class. Students can always count on a celeb or two parroting their cause. This is where you three really play a part. With your diplomatic immunity and your assignments at the embassy, your presence at these campuses shouldn't draw too much attention. Obviously Roland has the strongest position here as the guy who is supposed to liaise with the educational systems between the two countries. Do you have any professors you can identify who would be sympathetic to the cause?"

Austin paused a moment and then said, "Yes, of course. Like most people in education, they hate their government. However, most lean way far to the left and wish to see a full-fledged communist state."

"The enemy of my enemy is my friend," Andy quoted the age-old cliché. "Besides, everyone knows that American organized labor is socialist—some even promoting communism.

Look at the head of the USW. He claims to be a registered communist. And what is CLU but the international arm of US unions? Use that, if need be, to persuade." Andy stopped for a moment and then added, "Hell, I have pics of some SEIU members draped in the communist flag. I'll give them to you."

"In that case I could get a lot of support."

Andy turned to Dahlia next. "You're here to share best practices in agriculture. Not only does that give you entrée to the colleges and universities, it also gives you access to those farmer coalitions that are fighting the government over the land grabs. You have a perfectly good reason to be talking to both."

"I have some great processes for farmers involving cultivating twice as many crops from smaller amounts of acreage. I can use that to teach courses at the universities and also have town halls in order to share it with the rural people," Dahlia offered.

The most senior state department person was Roland, and Roland would have a bit of a problem in justifying his presence anywhere but at an oil field.

Roland smiled at Andy's dilemma for a moment and then laid out a solution. "Yes, the Gomez administration is not so happy with me right now, given our government's stand on the US company oil rigs their government seized, but I've been here awhile, and this is a normal bump in the road. However, it does open the door for me to introduce alternative energy sources a la renewables and to demonstrate to the college kids the wave of the future. After all, my title does encompass other energy, too. In fact, I could get my hands on some solar panels and set up experimental power-generating stations in the slums around Caracas. I can bring students there to help me, thereby creating an environment for the meeting of the minds, so to speak, or the birth of a partnership in a common goal. Where else can the two classes cross paths? My plan solves that problem."

Roland's self-satisfied smile showed how impressed he was with his own idea.

"Indeed it does," Andy replied. He glanced up and looked at the woman alone at the table again. *Still furiously texting.* His lips involuntarily pursed.

"Something wrong?" Joyia asked, seeing his look of concern.

"Does that woman over there look familiar to you?" Andy responded.

"Yes, she looks like any other tourist who comes to Brazil," Joyia responded.

Andy turned back to his binder and continued. "Second step—control the message. From the beginning, the government will promote the idea that opposition politicians are behind the student mobilizations, and the government-controlled media that covered one of the earlier student demonstrations in Plaza Brion in Chacaito would report that the political opponents of the party in power were instigating the demonstrations disguised as a student demonstration. Like the United States, Venezuela had its own powerful media machine. The press and talk radio were brutally efficient in either lifting a rebellion to popular cult status like Occupy

Wall Street or shrouding a movement with dark, sinister intentions. Just ask anybody in the Tea Party. But the one thing the American media always loves is a populist revolt. The working-class underdog against a heavy-handed imperialist regime. However, the Gomez government-controlled media does not harbor the same soft spot as the American press. There are a couple of news outlets in Venezuela that could be counted on. Regimes that fire on their own population always draw the ire of the mainstream media. We would need to count on the US media, with the help of the UK and France to overwhelm the airwaves with the 'right' view. Therefore, it's important that the State Department have someone stateside who can keep up a steady pace of press releases to feed the media beast. In fact, we need a whole PR campaign to roll this out. Be well aware that Gomez will be pointing to us first as instigators, and he'll rely heavily on our past record with the Chavez coup."

Roland nodded. As the most senior person at the table, he automatically took over as the lead spokesperson for the group from the embassy.

"Now, Francisco has already helped us with the third step, and that's identifying our poster child to give the movement the right face," Andy continued. "Francisco selected Cesar Lopez as his youth leader. He had the right first name. Cesar Lopez would bring up images of Cesar Chavez. He is very handsome in that dark Latino way, so the ladies would support him no matter what brush Gomez painted him with. Cesar has been a member of Un Nuevo Tiempo, a social democratic opposition party. So he was politically active and smart, and he's a young, hot-blooded Latino, passionate enough to die for his cause." Andy filled in the rest of the group, conveniently leaving out the part where Cesar had confided to Francisco that he would much rather live—and possibly slip into some nice political appointment maybe?

Again Andy looked around at everyone at the table to make sure there was comprehension. "All right, then," Andy said, seeing that they were all onboard. "Now, the fourth step is what we have already touched on earlier—a sympathetic media. Since Globovision was shut down back when Chavez was alive and spreading misery, we won't be able to count on any homegrown media help. However, just over the borders, Brazil and Colombia can be counted on. In a nutshell, once we have sufficiently agitated the masses, we give the signal, and Lopez would call for a press conference and encourage students to rise up, throw off the chains of oppression, and protest a government that was crushing the life out of the Venezuelan population. This is the most crucial and most dangerous step. We give the signal too soon, and Lopez is a dead man, and the revolution is over before it starts. Timing, people. It is all about timing and knowing the people you will be coordinating.

"Now, if everything goes well in this step we get to play the bonus round, which is step five. In this step we utilize the 'generals' of the movement. These student leaders have also been recruited by Francisco and Marco. They include Mark Lema, a university student with ties to Primero Justicia, and the aptly named Michelle Guevara, who belongs to the oddest of opposition organizations, Bandera Roja. BR is an ostensibly communist organization that made the improbable shift from a proper guerrilla group to the attack dogs of the Far Right, arguing that they were using the opposition as a means to collapse the false communism of Chávismo socialism and establish a proper dictatorship of the proletariat. Her name in itself is a good selling point. With the start of properly placed rumors, the world will speculate on a possible blood tie between her and the late, not-so-great Che Guevara. Hell, we should even promote that there is a blood tie between the two. Che was certainly a good tactician, which I admire, but the man was crude and lacked panache. Michelle does not suffer the same handicap. She's charming, smart, and has that innate talent of being able to get large groups of people to follow her. Your paths will cross."

"And how does this journey end?" Roland inquired.

"The finale?" Andy asked. "Well, I'm so glad you asked, Roland. There will be a small group of unnamed individuals who will remain in the background and pull the strings to make Paulo Mandura the next president of Venezuela. So say the Free World, so say we all!" Andy smiled a very cynical smile.

Eight

By the time Andy and Joyia returned to the hotel, the woman with the Amazon baseball cap was all but forgotten. She did not forget them, though. Not wanting to return to the hotel so quickly after they had, Denise scoped out an Internet café with Wi-Fi and entered. After paying the attendant for the password, Denise found herself a vacant table and connected her tablet to the Internet. The pictures that she had taken with her phone had automatically uploaded to her cloud, so she would be able to retrieve them using her tablet and send them in an e-mail attachment.

After sending the e-mail off to Peter, she dialed his number.

"Yes?" Peter asked when he answered.

"I just sent you pictures of two men and a woman who met with Andy and Joyia this morning. I need IDs, please, ASAP."

"OK," Peter responded, sounding ruffled.

"What about the photos I sent you last night?"

"Jesus, Denise, I'm the chief of staff, not the head of the CIA. Give me at least twenty-four hours."

"Peter, time is vital."

"Yes, yes. I'll hurry."

Denise hung up without the courtesy of saying good-bye. She then dialed the number of her contact at the SEBIN. Her call rolled over to voice mail, and Denise gave a disgusted sigh. No wonder countries were crumbling beneath the feet of those who ruled. They were completely oblivious to the dangers, so sure that their places on top of the mountain were secure. She shook her head in loathing.

Denise gathered her things and slipped into the restroom of the café to shed the trappings of her simple disguise. She stuffed them into the garbage can before she left the restroom. She would not be wearing them again. It had been about thirty minutes since Andy and Joyia had left their morning meeting. Denise had followed them at a distance only to the point where she had been sure that their destination was the hotel. Now she headed there herself.

The afternoon sun was high in the blue sky, and the humidity made the air heavy like a wet blanket. No wonder people in this part of the world retreated inside for a siesta. The combination of heat and humidity was oppressive and turned a tropical paradise into a punishing sauna. Denise felt the sweat roll down her back as she walked the short distance to the hotel. A shower would be the first thing on her list when she got into her room.

She felt the air conditioning of the lobby hit her like an icy wall as she entered the hotel. She made her way to the elevators and pushed the button for her floor. She stepped out on her floor and stopped just outside Andy's door. She heard a low murmur of voices and turned to her door, letting herself into her room.

Andy was studying what he was working with and found something lacking. "I need someone in Colombia. I need a backup. The logistics here will be tricky." He frowned as he continued to scratch out notes on his notepad.

"Those people from the State Department, they're not really with the State Department, are they? CIA maybe?" Joyia prodded.

Andy didn't even look up from what he was doing. "They are attached to the embassy, Joyia. That's all you need to know. I have confidence in Austin and Roland, but I can't believe they sent me a rookie like Dahlia with so much at stake." Andy felt flustered. "I need to call Koshka. Why don't you run out and see if you can get these things on my list? Also, find out what our options are to get over the border." Andy handed her a roll of reals and sent her out to the city.

This process would not happen overnight, Andy realized. It would take time. Sending a whole country into open rebellion against its government was not something that could be expedited on a whim or carried out by amateurs. Still, the fires would be easy to light in Venezuela since they had been burning since the Chavez coup. No, not just burning but also growing. But to get this rebellion off as quickly as possible and without the same result as last time, Andy decided he needed to make the call and ask Koshka to send someone to the CLU field office in Colombia. Andy needed Dane. He didn't care for the man personally, but he was the best person for what Andy would need out of Colombia.

Nine

Koshka sat staring out her office window at the bustling Washington, DC, streets. Her gaze shifted south toward Venezuela as her phone started to ring.

"Koshka, it's your favorite employee," Andy's voice greeted her.

Koshka grimaced at the thought. "What's going on, Andy?"

Andy gave a quick summary of what was happening and the fact that the CIA had sent a rookie field agent. He voiced his concern and the fact that it just basically pissed him off.

"Koshka, the bottom line here is if you expect to pull this off in the next few months—quite an expedited process, I might add, for such an endeavor—then I need another very experienced operative. I need Dane in Colombia. I'll need Colombians in the streets, I'll need Colombians in uniform, and I'll need someone else with a brain."

"Well, Andrew, I don't want you to blame me if you fail, so I'll give you what you ask for. And you're in luck. Dane has just returned," Koshka replied in her best patronizing voice. She knew that Andy was stewing on the other line of the phone. He hated being called Andrew.

"I'll have Dane fly into Bogota," she went on. "He can get organized there. Last intel I had, there was a decent-sized population of Venezuelan expats just over the border in Colombia. Most are political activists who went there to escape Chavez and haven't returned. I'll give Dane everything he needs. Perhaps they can be mobilized. Our office in Bogota will know more."

"Thank you, Koshka."

"I'll have Dane touch base with you when he lands in Bogota. Good luck." With that, Koshka hung up and pressed the intercom on her phone. "Agnes, get Dane in here, ASAP."

Dane was another operative who had returned last week from northern Africa. He had entered the building earlier that morning to catch up on the local politics that had been moving along at an ever-changing pace since he left.

Koshka knew this because she knew everything there was to know about her agents. Dane had always been a political junkie when it came to both office and national politics. He had a sharp mind and was not as laissez-faire about the world as Andy Wayne. In fact, quite the opposite—Dane was seriously inquisitive and a strategic thinker, when military planning was involved, in a way Andy was not. They were two different sides of the same coin, and there was some animosity between them. Despite this, the two made a perfect team and had a grudging respect for each other. Andy was the perfect union organizer, the perfect front man. He could sell any dream to any group of people at any time. He could motivate them to go to great lengths to achieve their dreams. Andy was a supremely gifted orator and, when you stripped away the glitz, a talented salesperson.

Dane wasn't even close to Andy's caliber in that department. The somber, dark-eyed mulatto with the aquiline nose excelled at taking what Andy had started and turning it toward something more substantial once the revolution had been sparked. Unlike Andy, Dane was an accomplished craftsman. Dane was an excellent general in leading the troops. He was not afraid to get his hands bloody. Andy was not afraid of blood; he just felt it was beneath him, and he was lazy. That was why Dane was the perfect counterbalance to Andy. Andy promised a dream to revolutionaries, and Dane managed the nightmare that was left behind by the sudden absence of a central government. And now those critical aspects of Dane's talents were exactly why Koshka needed him.

Koshka didn't have to wait long to hear the firm rap at her office door followed by Dane stepping through. Koshka had a bond with Dane she did not share with Andy. She understood Dane. He was so much like her. She could see him leading CLU one day, but he still had much to learn. Koshka nodded to one of the soft, leather-bound chairs on the opposite side of her desk, and Dane gracefully settled in. She studied him for a minute. His movements were elegant in their efficiency. He was lethal, and his whole being exuded that air.

Just as she studied him, he was studying her. Koshka was not the enigma to him she presented to others. Her toned body told him that even at her age, she was capable of removing someone from her path. Her movements communicated that she still maintained a level of expertise in what once must have been how she earned her living.

He scrutinized her expression, but even to him, her intent was hidden. On more than one occasion, his mind had played out the fantasy of having her under him, although she was fifteen years his senior. She brought to mind the words from a Gordon Lightfoot song his father liked so much: "She's a hard-loving woman got me feeling mean." She brought that out in him. Of that there was no doubt. He wanted to not just have her under him but to be in control. Dane smiled at the image. It was a sensuous fantasy, not born from a desire to hurt but reaching back to something more primal.

Koshka's voice broke through his musings.

"I need you to go to Bogota, Colombia, to partner with Andy. It seems the CIA's assistance is less than stellar. Andy also wants a two-pronged rebellion with aid from our office in Colombia. The time we have allotted for this makes it hard to do this solo. Also, I didn't tell Andy this, but I have it from a very good source that he has found himself in the crosshairs of a very foolish woman. I don't want Andy to lose his focus on what he's doing because he's more worried about a possible target on his back." She pushed a piece of paper across the desk to him. "His location is on that paper. As well as contact information. I've instructed Agnes to gather all the information that Andy has as well as information about the current setup at the Bogota office."

Dane glanced at the paper and then pushed it back toward her. His photographic memory came in handy. "Who's the woman?"

"One of Peter Abercrombie's little minions. If it's convenient, feel free to contain her in a permanent manner. But don't put yourself at risk. Venezuela needs to be in the full throes of a civil war as soon as possible. These windows of opportunities do not open often, and they close quickly. Oil prices are plunging, but that can reverse at any time. Gomez cannot get help from Russia because of the same problem—low oil prices. South America can be ours. Move fast, Dane. This time we should carry the day and have the occasion to spit on Chavez's grave. Eventually, I'll need you to go there to assist in putting the new government together and help the new leader cement his grip over the country. I don't need you put yourself at any unnecessary risk."

"How did we get the tip? And are you planning to ever tell Andy?"

"I was actually going to tell him today, but then I decided to hold back since I was sending you there. You and Joyia are much better at handling these things than Andy. After you're there and assess whether there really is a threat, you're free to tell him. Use your judgment. Joyia's contact information will be in the folder Agnes is putting together for you. The tip is from someone who has provided us with reliable information in the past about White House activities. They happened to overhear a phone conversation." Koshka offered nothing further.

Unlike Andy, Dane did not ask any additional questions. He knew Koshka well enough to know that she had provided him with more than enough to do his job, and any additional questions would only provoke her.

Also unlike Andy, Dane's flight to the El Dorado International Airport in Bogota was easily booked on Delta, and he wouldn't even have to switch airlines. An early morning flight out would get him into Bogota at about 11:00 p.m. The best part was that there was a Marriott in Bogota, and Dane happened to be a Marriott Platinum member.

Traveling had its advantages. Dane preferred chain hotels. You could count on a certain standard. Even better, they had an airport shuttle. He liked efficiency and hassle-free arrangements when he could get them. He picked up the folder from Agnes on the way out of Koshka's office and planned on reviewing it on the flight down to Colombia.

He grabbed what he needed from his office and headed out the door to his Foggy Bottom condo. He had some packing to do. He even allowed himself to start thinking about Joyia Gabriella. No doubt she and Andy had already enjoyed a lusty reunion. Perhaps he, too, could look forward to the same reunion. She was just as committed to a more carnal cause as she was to the one-world revolution. Dane allowed himself a small smile as he walked out into the DC sunlight.

Koshka decided she needed some air—a chance to clear her mind and have a fresh look at the opportunity that Cuba presented. Now that Andy had help on the way, she could have a more introspective study of what it was she should do regarding Ezekiel's insistence of starting another populist revolution in Cuba. Honestly, how much of the world did the Board want in flames at the same time?

Although CLU afforded her the choice of having a driver, Koshka preferred to do her own driving. She enjoyed the activity, and she was overly private when it came to her personal dwelling. Koshka did not invite visitors or even encourage people to just "drop in." Her private abode was the only place where Koshka could let her guard down. She discouraged social calls.

As she grabbed her briefcase and purse, Koshka made a note to send Joyia a bonus. While the lusty Latina enjoyed indulging in the pleasures of the flesh, Koshka knew that she had just put her in the unenviable position of balancing between two alpha males with very healthy sexual appetites.

Koshka gave a nod to Agnes as she exited her office. "I'll be out of pocket for the rest of the weekend, Agnes, unless there's an emergency."

"Very well, Miss Whitehall," Agnes responded.

Agnes was another indication of Koshka's personality, which liked structure and rspect for a chain of command. Agnes was a Brit and believed in a stiff upper lip and all that. She never asked questions that she felt were above her station. She zealously guarded the gate that gave access to Koshka, and she was a model of prim, proper competence.

Agnes had been a member of the British Labour Party prior to her relocation to the United States. When Koshka first inherited her position, the first thing she did was transfer all those who were in the inner office of the previous director out of the inner office. She didn't want any old loyalties casting a shadow over her reign. She wanted someone who was committed to the cause and whose first loyalty would be to her. She was not looking for someone who was friendly and outgoing. She didn't want a pal or even the illusion of a pal. Agnes fit the bill.

Koshka met her at a labor conference just before she assumed the director's mantle. Agnes was a shrew of a woman. She was just turning fifty when she met Koshka and bitterly fighting to be recognized as having so much more to offer the cause. Agnes bore a plain countenance with wispy gray hair. On the surface, her pinched expression and unsmiling face gave people pause when they approached her. Koshka saw past all that and only saw what Agnes had to offer.

And what Agnes brought to the table was a stout physique, a no-nonsense approach to running an office, and a devotion to her boss that was borderline idol worship. Koshka liked to be worshipped. For Agnes, Koshka gave her what she had been looking for: a purpose. Her kingdom was the inner sanctum of Koshka Whitehall, executive director of the CLU. As such, she carried her own influence. No one could see or talk to Koshka without going through Agnes. It was a responsibility that Agnes took on with ferocious tenacity. Soon after settling in as director, Koshka made Agnes an offer that Agnes could not, would not refuse. They had been together ever since.

Koshka left her office, located just a stone's throw from the White House, and headed toward I-66 and the Potomac River Freeway. From there she got onto the George Washington Memorial Parkway North. She drove slightly above the speed limit—nothing that would attract the attention of law enforcement. It wasn't until she exited onto VA-267 W that she pressed her foot a little heavier on the gas pedal.

Forty-eight miles from her office, Koshka reached her private nirvana. Her home was a charming, custom-designed structure nestled on twenty-five acres of tranquility. It was not ostentatious, but it had vaulted ceilings and an open, airy feel. It was a little over 3,700 square feet of cream-colored walls with bamboo and terracotta tile. Brightly colored works of art added a flair that kept it from being plain. Skylights guided shafts of sunlight throughout the home. The cozy-looking house displayed a wraparound porch and private upper decks with serene views of the Virginia countryside.

Koshka's great love was her horses. Her private retreat was equipped with a three-stall stable that also offered a tack/feed room and loft. The surrounding acreage contained three paddocks, surrounded by weather-stained board fencing, and a large riding ring.

The undeveloped acres that remained held a riding trail and a stone bridge over a bubbling creek. A private road led to the house, which was hidden from travelers on the main road, and emptied into a circular driveway and a two-car garage.

This little piece of paradise was located just outside the village of Waterford, Virginia.

Koshka had given careful consideration to the location she chose to call home when she relocated to Virginia over a decade ago. It needed to be secluded, small, and close to DC. There was an irony in the selection that amused her. Lyndon LaRouche had made his home in the early 1980s in the neighboring town of Leesburg. She remembered him well and owed him much. She had made her bones with the Board by taking part in a small operation that would eventually break the back of his right-wing organization. It was amazing how close that man got to the truth about the government. Five years in a federal prison cured him of continuing down that path.

Koshka changed into a pair of jeans and a sweater to guard against the late afternoon chill. Grabbing three apples, she headed out to the stable where her two best friends hung out. Smokey's Rio Grande was a coal-black horse with a white snip on her forehead. She stood at just a little over fifteen hands and was a double-registered quarter horse. She had been shown in her early years, but the eight-year-old mare had not been on the rail, as they say in the horse-show business, for three years now. In the stall across from Rio was Grand Commander Slam, a twelve-year-old paint gelding. His coloring was stunning: white backdrop with splashes of steel gray dramatically accented by a thick black mane and tail.

Side by side, the pair was exquisite. In the stall next to Slam was a miniature horse named Mini Me. Mini Me's sole job was to keep whichever horse was left behind company. One time, several years ago, when Koshka had first bought Rio, she had ridden out on Slam. The cacophony that followed was overwhelming as Rio proceeded to kick down her stall door, not happy to be left behind. Hence the search for a companion that culminated with the arrival of Mini Me.

This time, Koshka led Rio out. Rio could not be put into crossties without the risk of her coming unglued. Koshka would have loved to know the story on that, but in deference to the horse's fear, she dropped the lead rope, and Rio stood still as Koshka ran a currycomb over the mare's body.

Once out on the trail, Koshka allowed the mare to pick the path as she zoned out, contemplating what course of action she should take with Ezekiel and the Board.

The fall weather reinvigorated Koshka, and she allowed her mount to set the pace on the path that wound through her property. Her mind had assembled the outline of a plan of action to respond to the White House chief of staff's apparent attack on her people and her task. A task assigned to her by the Board, no less! Of course, if Denise had managed to actually do damage, Koshka would have to ratchet up the penalty phase a bit.

Her phone interrupted her thoughts. The unwelcome sound reverberated within the heavily wooded area. The ringer was set to Fire and Ice, the theme song to *Game of Thrones*. Koshka loved irony.

"Yes." She was all business, short and direct.

The voice on the other end was familiar to her. It was the COO of the Board. His smooth contralto voice filled her ear.

"Koshka, Cuba seems ready for intervention."

"We seem to have a bit of a snag in Venezuela," she responded.

"I'm sure you are more than capable of dealing with that."

"I am capable of many things, but coping with our present administration is not among them. If it wasn't for Christophe's indecision and paranoia, we could have brought the Arab spring to a successful conclusion. Because of his weakness, we've had to watch Russia, with its usual brutish and clumsy tactics, try to push the US out of its leadership role."

"In what way has Russia endangered our mission?" she heard his calming, self-assured voice ask.

"Parking a military ship in Cuba; threatening Estonia, Poland, and the Czech Republic—let alone the path they have cut through the Ukraine. Others in NATO have allowed this! They are more intimidated by Russia than they are us."

"Russia is a bumbling oaf in the ways of diplomacy. Its actions have only angered others. The Board will only tolerate it so long. They cannot think to blackmail the Board into submitting to its wants like a spoiled child."

"But the Board is made up of NATO members. Why are they allowing these aggressions?"

"Koshka, you yourself recognize that no government will stand that its own people or others fear. They are constantly plotted against until they fall. It's inevitable. When the real choice is put before the representatives on the Board, do you think they'll choose an oppressive fist hovering over them, using threats to keep them in line, or a benevolent leader, who offers a helping hand and tolerates minor transgressions?"

"I see the point and understand your logic, but—"

Koshka was interrupted by that soothing voice again. "Koshka, I gave you so much more credit than you are showing me now. Russia is being economically starved. Is that not the best way? We can smile and tolerate their lack of diplomacy, even their aggression against other countries, and allow them to think we have become nothing more than a weak-kneed giant while surreptitiously draining their country of all its economic strength. Do you think Reagan was the only one who could destroy Russia by bankrupting her?"

"My apologies, and you are right. I am afraid my temper is getting the better of my judgment," said Koshka.

"The president and all those he surrounds himself with may be oblivious to what happens in the real world, but he is not the first one like this. It is why we were created and why we operate outside of politics."

Koshka tried once more. "I just don't want this to go the same way as the Arab spring. Especially with Cuba on our back porch. I'm afraid if we move too fast, the president and his sycophants will freeze in terror like babes in the woods. He was not onboard with Venezuela. In fact, he wanted us to stand down."

"Venezuela will kick off a hot Latin summer. Cuba will follow. There is no inch of give on this decision with the Board."

Koshka said nothing because there was nothing to say. The Board wanted to move on Cuba. The Arab spring was now transforming into a hot Latino summer—or winter, depending on your geographic location.

The COO went on. "There is also something simmering out West—northern Nevada, Wyoming, Idaho, Utah, and the eastern parts of Washington and Oregon."

"Imagine that," Koshka responded with a touch of sarcasm.

The silence on the other end told Koshka she had just strayed too close to being disrespectful. But being Koshka, she didn't apologize. It would have been insincere, and they both knew it.

"Yes, do imagine it, Koshka," the COO said when he finally spoke. "And when you are through with imagining it, get someone out of the AFL-CIO that you trust to go and keep an eye on the extremists."

"Of course."

The beep indicating another call was coming in registered with Koshka, but she pushed it into the back of her mind until her call with the COO had ended.

"Koshka," the COO said quietly, "you will have your vengeance. Be patient. When the time is right."

Ten

Roland, Austin, and Dahlia arrived back in Caracas with a new level of energy. The last-minute directive sending them to Boa Vista was when they knew that whatever was going to happen was happening now. All of them felt a spike in their adrenalin after they left the meeting with Andy and Joyia. Now, back in Caracas, they had their own plans to make. It was up to them to assist Francisco in ginning up the college students. Dahlia would also venture into the rural area to spur on the discontent among the farmers and to set up communications with rural populations and the students so they could coordinate. It was a tall order for a rookie.

There were ten major cities in Venezuela, one in each state, with Caracas, the capital, being the largest. The three of them would not be able to cover all ten. It would therefore be important to connect with Francisco and Marco to see what assistance they could give. Andy would also be making his way into Venezuela, along with Joyia, but they would definitely have to rely heavily on the community organizers for all the factions. In reality, they would provide support and encouragement as well as any supplies that they could realistically provide, but they had to remain in the background.

Roland spoke once the three of them had settled into the secure room in the embassy. This room was swept every day for bugs and listening devices. Its walls were soundproof, so they risked no breach of security while they talked. "Austin, I think it'd be best for you to reach out to Marco and see what connections he can help you with inside the universities. Start here in Caracas."

Austin nodded.

"Once Caracas is set up then we can move out toward the other cities. We prioritize by population size. Largest first. Dahlia, you move in the opposite direction. Start with Petare, in Miranda. That's the smallest city out of the ten, and you can connect with the farmers and the students at the universities there. Since agricultural groups are your primary focus, you go from small to large. Maybe Francisco or Marco could help us there. I'll make my first mission Maracaibo, in Zulia."

The other two at the table did not dispute Roland's directions. The next day they started. There was no time to be lost.

Within the next two days, all the CIA/Embassy diplomats had made the contacts they needed to make in their first assigned city. And then Dane landed in Bogota. He hit the ground running.

Dane's first move was to reach out to Joyia. She picked up on the first ring. "*Hola. Como esta?*" she answered, not recognizing the number.

"Joyia, its Dane. Are you somewhere you can talk?"

"Dane, my handsome American. I can talk. Andy, he is in his room working, and I sit alone in my room." She played at pouting.

"I bet this is the first time you've used that room since Andy arrived," Dane joked.

"Are you jealous that some other man has had his wicked way with me?" Joyia teased.

"No," Dane parried. "Just trying to see how much work has been done and how much has just been fun. After all, I'm here to pick up the slack."

"You Americans—always so uptight. Work, work, work." She laughed. "Where are you, my handsome American? Are you helping us free our brothers and sisters from the chains of Chavismo?"

"Nothing so honorable. I'm here to help Andy fulfill the directives of CLU. And I need you to keep an eye out. Andy seems to have come into the crosshairs of someone hired to retire him permanently. I don't know if this is just gossip or fact, so I need you to keep your eyes open. It would be very sad if something happened to Andy and I was your only go-to guy left to bed from America."

Joyia let out an exuberant guffaw. "Yes, this is so true. You are too intense. I need the fun. I like many flavors."

"Joyia, don't tell Andy yet. I'll let him know once I see how far along we are," Dane advised.

"I can do that. Will I see you soon?"

"You'll see me eventually. I'm in Bogota right now. Once we get coordinated at the CLU office here, I'll be heading out to Macaio. I think that it'll be easier for me to work through the Zulia State. The governor, as well as the people, are very anti-Gomez. I should find a lot of people there who'll help me get what I need through that border area."

"They hated, Chavez, too when he was alive," Joyia added. "Be careful, Dane. That is an area heavy with drug traffickers and other *banditos*."

"That's me, Mr. Careful," Dane responded. "Remember, keep your eyes open, and report to me anything that draws your attention."

"Si, I will. You know, the other day, when we met up with those people attached to your consulate in Venezuela, there was a woman there at the restaurant who caught Andy's attention. I don't know why. She was a *gringa*. She looked like a tourist, but for some reason, she made Andy uneasy."

"Did he say why?"

"No, no, he couldn't figure out why she bothered him, either. He did not recognize her." Joyia paused. "But he did ask me about her. Perhaps there is something there. Perhaps not, though."

"Listen, Joyia, if you see her again, you need to let me know. Get a picture of her if possible. What did she look like?"

"Nothing special. Couldn't really tell. She had a ball cap on with her hair tied behind her head. Brown hair. Hmmm, she was sitting down, so I couldn't say how tall she was. She had on a poncho. One of those the locals make to sell to tourists, but it was big and loose, so I do not know if she was skinny or fat."

Dane was quiet a moment and then said, "OK. Listen. Keep your head down and eyes open. I'll talk to you soon."

With that, Dane cut the connection. The woman in the restaurant made him uneasy, too. Andy was no amateur. Sure, he was a prima donna, but the man had been in the game a long time. His sixth sense was well developed. Dane would bet his last dollar that Denise was in Boa Vista.

Eleven

Denise was getting restless. Andy had not come out of his room for three days. She did not know how the man operated, but obviously he liked solitude while planning. His only visitor was Joyia. She provided some company and brought food. Other than that, there was no sign of life. Denise had gotten a response from her contact in Venezuela and now had names to put on the two Latinos who met Andy at the pub her first night in Boa Vista. The Venezuelan authorities knew them to be antigovernment activists and had been keeping an eye on them. However, they hadn't done anything to warrant being arrested. Her contact assured her that they would keep a closer eye on them now that CLU was in the picture.

Denise looked around her room, bored. Surely, he would come out of his room soon. She was going stir-crazy. By staying in his room, he was keeping Denise from getting in a good kill shot. She wasn't a sadist. She preferred a quick, clean shot to the head. In and out, preferably, though her slugs would not be traceable to her. She didn't like the idea of killing anyone else unless it was absolutely necessary to fulfill her contract.

Her reverie was disturbed by the ringing of her phone. She quickly answered it.

Peter didn't bother with pleasantries. "The photos of those three people you sent me? They are all three attached to the American embassy in Venezuela."

"CIA," Denise stated flatly. "I figured as much. Wanted to make sure."

"Yeah, well, I sent you the files that the State Department has on them so you can get an idea of what they are supposed to be doing down there. It should be in your e-mail."

"Great, I got it from here," Denise said.

"Well, give me an update," Peter insisted.

"Not much to tell. He's holed up in his room. Has been for the last three days. It's driving me crazy. I can't get at him."

"Does he know you're there? Perhaps he spotted you? Maybe he was tipped off about you."

"Well, Peter, unless you tipped him off, I'd say that there's a pretty good chance that he doesn't know about me. He doesn't know what I look like, so even if he saw me, he wouldn't know what he was looking at. That Brazilian bitch is acting pretty normal, so I assume this is how he works."

"Well, you figure it out. That's what you're paid to do." Peter sounded petulant.

"Yeah, well, I always do, don't I, Peter?" Denise clicked off the phone and went to retrieve the files from her e-mail.

Denise sat cross-legged on the bed as she read each file. Two of them she recognized, but the third one was unfamiliar to her. She read into Dahlia's file some more and exclaimed out loud, "A rookie, they sent a rookie!"

Denise chortled gleefully. Andy must have been really pissed when he found that out. Having come from the CIA, Denise was familiar with the general mode of operation. All three of them had a reason to interact with the public. All three of them had a reason to interact with special-interest groups. These three were the liaisons between Andy and the revolution. They would be offering hands-on technical support to Marco and Francisco. Denise decided that Andy was not going to be the wizard behind the curtain pulling strings in the revolution.

She grabbed her phone and dialed her contact in Venezuela.

"I've got the best gift for you, my friend," she said without waiting for him to speak.

"*Senorita, muy bueno* to hear you," a heavily accented voice replied. "What you got for me?"

"Your next promotion," Denise offered. "You'll owe me so much."

"And I always give the favor back."

"Yes, you do. I'll be sending three files to you via e-mail. There are three CIA operatives attached to the consulate there. They met with CLU several days ago here in Boa Vista, the morning after Marco and Francisco met with Andy. Very coincidental, don't you think?"

Denise was not expecting him to reply, and he didn't. He stayed silent as he waited for her to divulge the information that she wanted to share.

"Those three people will be CLU's CIA conduit to all the groups they need to light the fire on their revolt. You'll find the woman reaching out to the farmers and ranchers. You know, the same people whose land your government keeps confiscating. According to this file, she's been currently tasked with sharing agricultural practices in the rural area surrounding Pedre. Another is assisting universities in Caracas with involving student groups in the educational process and the forming of a Greek system." Denise laughed. "Good God, we certainly couldn't have a completely rounded education without sororities and frat parties."

Still her contact was silent. Denise did like center stage.

"The last one is doing outreach, but it doesn't say where. I'm sure you can find him. He's helping build bonding moments in the oil and energy sector. Of course, with the price of oil in the tank, your country should probably look at renewables." Denise could be very acidic when she wanted to.

Her contact finally spoke. "Yes, the oil prices are the cause of much concern. Without the money for oil, we cannot pay for the things Venezuela needs. The people here are very upset."

"Well, that's why your country is ripe for a coup. Tsk, tsk, you should diversify more, *mi amigo*," Denise cooed.

The face of the man on the other end of the phone scrunched up in anger, but when he spoke, he only agreed with her.

"*Gracias* for the files. Senorita, you are a true friend to Venezuela."

"Remember that, will you, if I should ever need a place that won't extradite?" Denise shut the phone. Now she only had to wait. The good news was that the Venezuelan government would move quickly.

And they did.

Dahlia was hosting a town-hall meeting with landowners on the campus of one of the private universities in Petare. The room was packed. And although the visual aids—posters, flipcharts, and the PowerPoint slide on the screen—promoted new irrigation techniques, the conversation was about more violent methods of keeping their land from the government.

Those in the room were surprised when the doors were thrown open and a small detachment of *federales* came into the room.

When the landowners stood up to confront the intruders, the officers quickly drew their weapons.

They gave orders in rapid Spanish to the crowd, and although the farmers and ranchers did not sit down, they didn't advance, either.

"Senorita," The officer in charge commanded Dahlia's attention. "You are under arrest for instigating insurrection." He reached out to grab her arm, but though she was a rookie, her training kicked in, and she twisted out of his reach. Dahlia had his arm behind his back without even thinking about the process. He grunted in pain.

"Don't you touch me, asshole." She yanked his arm up harder. "I have diplomatic immunity."

Another voice from somewhere to her left spoke up. "Yes, but he does not, Senorita."

She looked in the direction of the words and saw another officer with his gun placed against the head of one of the farmers.

With a sigh of resignation, she dropped the arm of the first officer. She didn't even see his fist coming, but she felt it connect. Her head snapped back as she felt the crunch of teeth. She lay on the floor, stunned momentarily. Groaning, she rolled to her side and spit out the fragments of teeth mixed with blood. She felt the air whoosh out of her lungs as his shoe slammed into her stomach.

"Senorita, your police may have to act like babysitters in America, but here there is no such thing as police brutality." He signaled to the back of the room, and two of the lower-ranking federales came up and took custody of her and lifted her from the floor.

At the same time that Dahlia was getting her first experience with police enforcement according to current Venezuelan custom, Austin was sitting with students among the beautifully maintained grounds of a private university in Caracas. Universidad Católica Andrés Bello (UCAB) was one of the biggest universities in Venezuela. It had campuses in several cities: Caracas, where the main campus was located, and Los Teques, Guayana, and Coro. The university was named in honor of Andrés de Jesús María and José Bello López, a Venezuelan humanist, diplomat, poet, legislator, philosopher, educator and philologist, whose political and literary works constitute an important part of Spanish-American culture.

It was the number-one Venezuelan University, according to the QS ranking, and the sixty-fourth in Latin America. The school motto was "*Ut innotescat multiformis sapientia Dei*" or "To make known the manifold wisdom of God," which was what Austin was attempting to do at that very moment.

Most of the students who attended the university came from the upper classes and more affluent middle-class families, although the university did have a robust scholarship program that enabled many from the poverty-stricken areas to attend. The educational reform that Austin was vigorously imparting to his rapt audience was more about the overthrowing of an oppressive government wrapped up in the mesmerizing retelling of the American Revolution.

"It was Patrick Henry who said the famous words, 'Give me liberty or give me death,'" Austin said with passion born from an avid love for the history of the war and his country's forefathers. He went on as he noticed the fire burning in the students' eyes. They were enthralled with the idea of a revolution that would erase the corruption rampant in their government.

Austin looked at the increasingly large group of students, and in carefully measured words, he quoted from memory a letter that Thomas Jefferson had written to the congress after the American Revolution: "God forbid we should ever be twenty years without such a rebellion. The people cannot be all, and always, well informed. The part which is wrong will be discontented in proportion to the importance of the facts they misconceive. If they remain quiet under such misconceptions, it is a lethargy, the forerunner of death to the public liberty. We have had thirteen states independent eleven years. There has been one rebellion. That comes to one rebellion in a century and a half for each state. What country ever existed a century and a half without a rebellion? And what country can preserve its liberties if their rulers are not warned from time to time that their people preserve the spirit of resistance? Let them take arms. The remedy is to set them right as to facts, pardon, and pacify them. What signify a few lives lost in a century or two? The tree of liberty must be refreshed from time to time with the blood of patriots and tyrants." He paused a moment to allow his words to cascade through the minds of an already rebellious youth. "Do you understand what he was saying in his letter?"

The students' gazes locked with his in silence. Austin continued. "The letter speaks volumes about what Jefferson, as well as other founding minds, thought with regard to the relationship between the citizens of a republic and their government. The relevance today, in my opinion, is pretty much what it was back then. Liberty can be lost unless the general populace maintains a constant vigil. And once liberty is lost, the only way to make the tree of liberty bloom again will be through the willingness to shed blood—your own and others'—so that freedom will once again grace its limbs and the people who live beneath it."

A hand from a student went up in the back of the crowd at the same time a police officer used his baton to hit the student in the back.

"Leave here now!" the officer ordered as the assaulted student cried out in pain. "Go now, all of you. You will be charged with sedition if you don't go back to your classrooms."

Other officers waded into the tight group of human flesh and start pushing and shoving the young adults gathered there. One student spoke up in protest and was quickly set upon by two baton-wielding officers, who left him rolling, bloody, on the lush lawn of the quad.

Austin rushed in at that point. "Get away from him!" he yelled at the police officers. "You bastards!"

Austin knew he would also get bloody for his trouble, but it was a beating he needed to take. He needed something to stick in the students' minds that would be unpleasant enough to galvanize them. "This isn't seditious! I was teaching them about American history, you assholes. Freedom of speech, you know? Learning."

He felt the first crack of the baton behind his knees, which easily brought him down to smash his face into the concrete walk. He heard a girl scream and the students scuffle with law enforcement as his body absorbed the blows from the officers standing over him. He had read about people who shut their minds down to the pain, and he decided that who-ever thought that was possible had never been beaten with billy clubs.

Although the thrashing only lasted a few minutes, in Austin's mind, it went on forever. When it was over, he could see, through one swollen eye, the students forming a loose ring around him. They parted to one side as the two officers holding his arms dragged him through the opening. The other officers had their guns out as a warning against further interference.

Roland was inside the consulate when the Ambassador's assistant came into his cubbyhole office. "Roland, the Venezuelan government has arrested Dahlia and Austin. They are transporting Dahlia back to Caracas as we speak. They have accused them and you of trying to promote a revolt, a government overthrow. President Gomez has requested that the ambassador come to the Palacio de Miraflores to answer to these accusations."

"Shit, shit, shit," Roland cursed. "I'll get all our things together. Are they in one piece?"

Roland was referring to the condition of his colleagues. The Venezuelan federales and police were known for their brutality.

"Don't know, but be prepared for the worst," the assistant responded as he left.

The American ambassador's meeting at the Palacio de Miraflores with President Gomez was not so much of a meeting as it was an hour of harsh accusations punctuated with threats. Threats to break off diplomatic relations, threats to go to war, and even the threat to build their own nuclear arsenal. The American ambassador apologized, using all of his talents as a diplomat. He sounded sincere and suitably humble.

"Get them out of my country!" Gomez had his face so close to the ambassador's that he covered the poor man with his spittle.

The ambassador mopped his face with a hanky as Gomez stormed out of the room, screaming, "Now!"

"Well, I guess this meeting is over," the ambassador said more to himself than to the gentleman who remained behind to escort him out of the palace.

At the American Embassy, the marines opened the gates as a black sedan with tinted windows pulled through. Inside were the battered but relieved attachés. They, like Roland, did not need to be told that they were being kicked out of the country. However, they had formal paperwork to drive the point home.

Twelve

Andy had a towel wrapped around his lower half as he stepped out of the shower. He leaned over the sink to trim his beard. His overall mood was a happy one. Everything seemed to be going smoothly. The key to any revolution was through good, solid organizing skills, which always required dependable captains to carry the message. It was impossible to be everywhere at all times. He had those captains in Marco and Francisco, and there were the three operatives at the consulate. Andy was pretty pleased with himself at the moment. He might not be able to pull this off by the deadline Koshka gave him, but it would be pretty damn close. Very close indeed. He started to hum an unrecognizable tune.

"Andy, come quickly," Joyia called from the hotel room. "Quick."

Andy came out into the hotel room where Joyia had the news on.

"They just said something about the American consulate in Venezuela," she said. "They said that they would talk about something happening there after the commercial break."

Andy walked over to the desk chair, sat down, and waited. Several minutes later the newscaster came back on the screen.

"In Caracas today, the US ambassador was called into a meeting with Venezuelan President Gomez over action by three people attached to the American consulate. The meeting was very tense, and President Gomez accused the American government of attempting to overthrow his presidency. At the end of the conference, Gomez gave three US diplomats forty-eight hours to leave the country, condemning them for conspiring against the Venezuelan government.

"The State Department spokeswoman stated that this was a desperate attempt to head off any rebellion that might result in riots. By casting blame and accusations on the American government, the Venezuelan government was hoping to stall any attempt by its own people to remove an oppressive regime. The world was aware of its repressive policies, and President Gomez was trying to garner sympathy by trying to turn public opinion against the US.

"The Venezuelan foreign minister said the three consular staff used visa visits to universities as a cover for promoting student-led protests. The US State Department called the allegations 'baseless and false,' adding that Washington supported free expression and peaceful assembly in Venezuela and around the world. Venezuela has routinely expelled US diplomats in recent years as the relationship between the two countries frayed during the fourteen-year rule of Hugo Chavez.

"Critics of the Venezuelan government in the international community dismissed such moves as theatrics used in times of national commotion to distract from more serious issues."

Gomez and his cronies might not have been as shrewd as Chavez, but even the most loutish government official could feel that the air was heavy with bloodlust. The pall that hung over Caracas was a hint of what would be the nation's most serious violence since President Gomez's election.

Andy's good mood evaporated quickly. This was a serious blow to his plans. Thank God he had had the foresight to pitch a bitch with Koshka and get Dane down here. He would certainly need him now. It also meant that Andy's plan to stay safely and comfortable ensconced in Boa Vista while the flames of revolution burned elsewhere was now in the trash can. He was going to have to go into Venezuela. However, with the latest expulsion and the country on the verge of a bloodbath, Americans would have a hard time getting into the country.

"Joyia, I've got to get in there. Find me a way."

"I know already of a way. We must go across the mountain."

"Are you shitting me? That would take forever."

"No, no, my handsome man, it is only a six-day trek. Marco and Francisco can keep it going for six days. The movement is strong now; we just need to fire the first shot of the revolution, and that would be more for Dane's group than ours."

Andy looked at her incredulously for a moment. His mind processed what she had been saying and realized that she was right. He needed to stop spinning his wheels for a moment and think. He had a sat phone, so he would be able to communicate if he rationed its use to save battery power. He could direct protests from afar. After all, that was what he was doing anyway. They could protest for six days until he got there with Dane on backup in case anything escalated while he was out living the life of a mountain goat.

Inwardly he groaned, though. Andy was not one for physical, outdoorsy adventures. He was an urban guy. This was more Dane's area of expertise. But, hell, it wasn't like he hadn't done this many times before in other countries with other revolutions.

He turned to Joyia. "Get it done. We need to leave tomorrow at first light."

Joyia left to make the arrangements, and Andy called Koshka.

She picked up on the first ring. She had been waiting for him to call. "Andy, I see you're making progress down there, but I thought we'd stay in the background," she said.

"My thoughts also. What's the fallout?"

"The world really doesn't care at this point. Venezuela is not high on anybody's buddy list. Europe is more concerned with Islamic extremists, and Russia is hiding its broken economy by beating up on the countries around it. China has no friends. They're immersed in getting a favorable trade deal with Russia for cheap oil. It's quite lovely in the world right now. No one is noticing your party down south. However, I did get a call from Peter Abernathy. Poor man seems distraught. Could not even contemplate what the president would say or how he would apologize." Andy could hear the contempt in Koshka's voice. "What happened?" she went on.

"I haven't a clue at this point. I'm making arrangements to get over the border and get things rolling myself. I'm going across the mountains. It'll take six days. I'll try to keep the sat phone up, but I may run out of battery juice. I gotta call Dane next and get him in the loop. He may have to move in from Colombia while I'm still in the mountains, so I want to make sure that he's hooked up with Marco and Francisco. I haven't even talked to him yet. He talked to Joyia, so he was read into the plan, and he was handling the fireworks for the event. He'll send in some uniforms during the second or third protest to offer up a martyr or two and send this into overdrive."

Although Andy could not see her, Koshka's head was nodding in agreement as she listened to him lay out the plan. "Sounds good," she said.

"Hey, this might throw us off schedule," he told her.

"Actually, I think this could be used to speed it up."

He heard a click signaling that she had broken the connection.

Thirteen

While Joyia was out making arrangements for their little trip that included meeting up with revolutionaries in the mountains, Andy started make the adjustments in the plans for a people's revolt. No one knew grassroots like American labor, and Andy smiled as he thought of the fact that he could agitate anyone in the world just by being what he was—an American. Andy came from the old school of union organizing. Koshka and her ilk might be the sophisticates of political chess, but Andy could organize a group of nuns into revolting against the church. He was just that good. That was why Koshka relied on him so heavily.

While the politicians and those with influence played the traditional political intrigues within the hallowed halls of the most powerful city in the world, Andy Wayne would get busy getting a revolution of the people off the ground despite the minor inconvenience of diplomats being expelled. Many would wonder why Venezuela would be of such interest to the superpower that employed Wayne. Yes, the United States was responsible for 40 percent of the exports from this country, and it was responsible for producing 30 percent of the imports going into Venezuela. That alone should have given the United States some diplomatic clout, but perhaps it was because the US diplomatic corps was woefully uneducated in the art of diplomacy that the government chose a more subversive method to implement its will.

It appeared that Gomez was enjoying a bonding experience with Iran and Cuba. The United States took one look at what was happening on the south end of the block and decided that the neighborhood was in serious jeopardy of going downhill fast. After all, everyone knows what happens to property values when the wrong kind of people move into the neighborhood. The rest of the world seemed to always be criticizing the United States' willingness to do battle, unless of course it was their own interests being threatened. Then it was "Where in the hell were you?"

So, in the tradition of his predecessors, Jay Lovestone and Irving Brown, Andy Wayne did covertly what the United States could not do overtly.

Andy picked up the phone and connected with Dane.

"What's up?" Dane answered.

"Did you hear what happened?" asked Andy.

"Yeah, we have TV over here."

"Look, I have to go across the border through the mountains. With the expulsion of the three amigos," Andy said, referring to Roland, Austin, and Dahlia, "the borders are going to be on alert. I can't risk any stops there."

"A mountain crossing? Do you think your Italian loafers will make it?"

"Fuck you," Andy shot back. Andy's failure to see the beauty of outdoor activities was well known throughout CLU, but he had done his fair share of endeavors out in the environment.

With the initial prickly exchanges out of the way, both men got down to talking business. Andy was high-strung, and his nerves frayed easily. Dane found this strange for someone in his profession, but the truth was that Andy liked the mind games. He was a junkie when it came to strategy and duplicity. He enjoyed winning over a rival through his intellect. Dane was always as cool as a cucumber. Nothing ruffled him. While he was not the chess player that Andy was, Dane found you could win just as many battles with brute force. Prior to coming onboard with CLU, Dane was in Special Forces, but his real claim to fame was his skill as a marksman. The two were opposite in every way except when it came to winning. Both were very competitive.

"You already have a copy of the plan I sent you in the e-mail. We stay the course with most of it. I'll just have to make some adjustments to fill the gap left by the consulate folks heading home. Where are you at on your end of the plan?"

"I'm in Macaio, right by the border into Zulia. I reached out to a few narco leaders that I came into contact with in my previous life, and they were able to help me out with the number of boots on the ground." Dane had friends who had left the military and set up shop as mercenaries. Many had become very affluent as private security for the Narco leadership in South America as well as Central America and Mexico. "I'm setting up camp here. It'll take a few days for everyone to check in. Otherwise, I'm in great shape. I have Venezuelan federales' uniforms, weapons, and everything in between. We should be able to rock and roll in three days."

"What's your placement of people?" Andy inquired. Although Andy was the lead on this campaign, he was smart enough to allow Dane to use his own strategy when it came to laying out their tactical planning. Dane was more the expert in that area.

"Initially we want to light it up starting in Zulia, because they're already at political war with Gomez. They are more likely to react the way we need them to. However, I already have my advance groups either in place or on their way to their locations across the country. Mostly the key cities like Caracas, Petare, and Maracaibo. They'll get into the Venezuelan uniforms and make appearances on the streets—you know, let everyone get familiar with their faces and accept them as federales. Once the people start protesting, those guys will make sure that the situation escalates. They know to look for journalists, photographers, and any local or national celebrities that come out in sympathy. They're biting at the bit for the party to start, so I can think of no problems at the present."

Andy often felt distain for Dane's "friends" and their eagerness for bloodshed. Not that he was against it. On the contrary, it was a necessary evil of the job, and he had often picked out those who would die. Like that poor sucker in Tunisia lighting himself on fire, which set off the overthrow of the Tunisian government. He just never understood the enthusiasm for it. In reality he thought that being the person who actually committed the killing was for those from a lower station in life, which was why he felt the dislike he did for Dane. He thought him common, not quite in Andy's same social circle.

"What happens if one them is arrested or killed?" The question was so amateur level that Dane could have easily been insulted, but he knew Andy needed to go through this to calm his nerves.

"Nothing to identify them. None are to be left alive. They travel in threes. If one is wounded and can't be carried out, they are to finish the job. However, should someone be taken alive, they have no idea who they're working for. They were just told that the head of the Narco family they work for is doing a favor for a friend."

"And what are the repayment terms for the favor?"

"The usual—a couple hundred kilos make it into the US without issue."

Andy accepted that. It was the usual deal with drug lords everywhere.

As the men continued to hash out the details, across the hall, Denise was so bored she could scream. She had to get out of her room. She had no reason to believe that Andy would be leaving anytime soon, so she grabbed her overly large sunglasses, added a floppy straw hat and headed out. She had just walked out onto the street when she noticed Joyia heading back to the room with three young boys following her, loaded down with purchases she had evidently made.

Denise ducked quickly into a pottery shop and watched the little entourage pass. Something was most definitely up. Denise followed at a reasonable distance as the group entered the hotel lobby she had just exited a few minutes before. They marched over to the elevators and began the trip up to the room. Denise found a comfortable spot in the lobby to wait for the three boys to make their way back down.

Her wait was not long. Fifteen minutes later, the elevator dinged and disgorged the boys. She made eye contact with the oldest of the three and signaled them over.

She didn't know if the boys spoke English, but she spoke fluent Spanish and explained her request to them. Her friends were planning a surprise for her birthday. The lady they had helped was one of those friends. She wanted to surprise them back, but in order to do that she needed to know what her friend Joyia had bought that morning. In an effort to cut to the chase quickly and skip any haggling, Denise held out three American five-dollar bills. The boys' eyes grew wide at such a sum of money. They would be rich!

"*Si, Senorita.*" The oldest went to snatch the bills, but Denise held them out of his reach.

"Tell me first," she said.

The boys did not believe for one moment the reason Denise wanted to know what the woman whom they had helped that morning bought. They didn't care. The money would go a long way in Boa Vista.

"She bought supplies to go hiking over the mountain," he said simply.

"Did she mention when she was going?" Denise asked.

"She paid a guide to meet them tomorrow morning before breakfast in front of the hotel. Juan has taken many over the mountain into Venezuela, so she made a good choice. You will be safe with him."

"Where in Venezuela?" Denise prodded.

"Santa Elena de Uairen."

"What type of vehicle does Juan drive?"

"A dirty white jeep." With that the boy succeeded in grabbing the money, and all three of them ran out the front doors of the hotel.

No, they won't be safe with him at all, Denise thought as she hurried out the hotel doors herself to get a few things she would need.

As Joyia unpacked the bags, Andy was finishing his call with Dane.

"Anything else, Dane?"

Dane briefly thought of the fact that someone was out there waiting to take a shot at Andy, but he decided against saying anything. Like Koshka, he wanted Andy to focus, and as he would be heading into the mountains, and Joyia hadn't noticed anyone suspicious hanging around, Dane felt that they should be relatively safe until they reached the populated areas of Venezuela just across the border. Venezuela's border areas, whether with Colombia or Brazil, could be treacherous because of the drug smuggling and other nefarious activities. More often than not, the police were either paid to look the other way or were directing the traffic of the contraband themselves. "I can't think of anything right now. Are you going to be out of contact?"

"I'll have the sat phone for as long as the battery holds out. I don't know if Joyia's cell phone will have a signal, but I'm kinda thinking that it won't. I'm told it's a six-day hike, so I'll try to reserve juice for as long as I can. I'll touch base at intervals and then shut it off."

Dane nodded as if Andy could see him. "Be safe, and keep your eyes open. Bad people running around out there."

Andy clicked off after assuring Dane he'd be careful. Joyia looked up from her task of sorting through the newly bought equipment when Andy walked over. "*Bueno?*"

"*Bueno*," Andy responded. "At least, I hope. Dane knows what he's doing. He has it covered."

Andy started examining the gear that Joyia had picked up for him. "What's the plan here, Joyia?"

"Juan will be coming in the morning to get us. We drive to the trailhead, and then he takes us across. We end up in Santa Elena de Uairen. It's a small town in Venezuela. It's the starting point for guided tours into the Gran Sabana. Very popular hike for tourists who do that sort of thing. When we get there, we can blend with the other groups, and they'll think that we're returning from hiking the Gran Sabana."

Andy nodded. With the exception of the fact he actually had to hike through a mountain pass, it was a pretty good plan. Chances of getting caught were slim in that environment.

"I got you a German passport. I remembered you said you spoke German. If they check you, can speak to them in

German. They won't know if you have an accent or not. *Dios*, they wouldn't even know you were speaking German. You could make up words they would not know," Joyia added.

Andy was impressed. Not only was she good in bed, she was efficient, too.

They turned in early as the idea was to make it to the trailhead by daybreak. Juan would be meeting them in front of the hotel just before breakfast.

Denise was also in bed early, but her alarm was set to awaken her just after three in the morning. She too had a plan in place. She would rise early and wait for Juan to pull up to the hotel. She would then place a tracking device on the vehicle while waiting for Andy and Joyia to come out. The device was magnetic, so it would be easy to place it inside a wheel well as she nonchalantly strolled by. She knew she couldn't just follow them out to the start-off point. Obviously there would be no traffic to hide in as she followed. It made sense to track them via a GPS. She would be starting out a couple hours behind them, but by traveling alone, she could make up time. She was in excellent physical condition. Her profession demanded it. She was also proficient with a compass and would carry her own Montana 650 device to help her find her way out of the mountains, along with a map of trails. After all, the idea was that she would be the only one who would come out of the mountains. Their deaths would be attributed to drug smugglers or other criminal elements that hung out around the border areas.

It was difficult to start hiking from the Brazilian side. The access was through the Raposa-Serra do Sol Amerindian reserve, where armed conflicts between the natives, rice farmers, and the authorities had been frequent. Most hikers chose to start ascending from the Venezuelan side. They would not actually scale Monte Roraima because, on the Brazilian side, it was nothing but a massive wall of granite. She was sure that the group would skirt the bottom and work its way into Venezuela through La Gran Sabana.

The massive region known as the Gran Sabana was sheltered by Canaima National Park. Canaima was enormous—approximately the dimensions of Belgium. It ranked among the world's biggest protected areas and was made a World Heritage Site over ten years ago. The Gran Sabana was a direct translation of "tei pun" in the Pemon Indian tongue, and roughly extended over the southeastern section of the park, where most Pemon were concentrated in various villages established in the 1940s and 1950s by Capuchin missionaries.

But no one from Andy's group or Denise herself would be paying much attention to the grandeur that was the Gran Sabana.

Fourteen

Denise twisted her head back and forth in an effort to keep from becoming stiff. As she took a sip of some lukewarm espresso, an off-white Jeep Wagoneer pulled up in front of the hotel.

Now there's a museum piece, she thought as she watched the driver hop out and go into the hotel. Denise couldn't believe her luck at having such an easy window of opportunity to place the tracking device on the vehicle. She almost clapped her hands with glee. These things don't happen too often. Denise quickly got out of the car and started toward the Jeep. It wasn't until she was almost on it that she noticed a head leaning against the passenger window.

Shit, she thought. Quickly changing her plan, Denise ducked behind the back of the Wagoneer and deftly placed the tracker up under the black painted bumper. She would have preferred to place it under a wheel well, but it is what it is.

As she made her way back into the shadowed alcove where the hotel attached to the neighboring building, Andy's voice wafted out through the opening door.

She couldn't make out what they were discussing as they loaded their gear into the back end of the vehicle. As soon as they were done, they just as quickly got into the four-wheel drive, made a U-turn into the street, and headed out of town.

Without wasting any time, Denise retrieved her rental car from the parking lot. She pulled out onto the main street and pulled over to the side. She set up the tracking system so she could clearly see the screen, even as she drove. She watched the red arrow that indicated her prey was on its way toward Venezuela.

Juan knew exactly where the perfect spot was for the three of them to start their journey. He had done this many times before. The main road from Brazil to Venezuela cuts through the eastern sector of the park, giving access to various points for them to turn off the road and hike out.

Juan turned toward Joyia and Andy, who were seated in the back seat. "This is my wife, Elena. She will drive the Jeep back to town after we unload everything. No one will know where we start out from."

Elena offered her hand to both of them. Remnants of beauty still clung to her pudgy face. She spoke no English, but her smile was genuine.

"Elena gave me seven beautiful sons," Juan boasted as he patted her hand. The two obviously still shared a loving relationship.

The Jeep sped down the highway, its strong engine belying the first impression it gave with its dented exterior. Somewhere, miles behind, Denise followed.

The sun was just sending tentative rays out to break through the dark when they reached their jump-off point.

They gathered their gear in front of the Wagoneer, using the headlights to see what they were doing. Andy double-checked the amount of moleskin packed into his backpack. His feet were going to be raw meat hiking in new boots.

The first day's seven-mile hike ascended rolling hills and vast grasslands through the Gran Sabana. Rain poured down during most of the hike, protecting the little group from the Equatorial sun. They stopped to fill water bottles from the same rivers and streams. The area was devoid of agriculture and livestock, so there was no risk of water contamination.

Around camp at night, the three shared stories in Spanish and English. Their laughter cut through the night air as Juan passed around a bottle of rum. In the morning, Juan and Joyia worked together, preparing fries, fritters, and eggs.

As they continued their journey, Andy couldn't help but admire the beauty of the area they were hiking through. Not long after they started out, they came to a river that wound its way through the Sabana.

"The river's low enough to cross," Juan advised. "Remove your shoes, because socks give a better grip on the rocks." Andy noticed a rope strung over the river and questioned Juan about it.

"We are not the only people who prefer to enter Venezuela this way, senor. You will need the rope to steady yourself during the crossing, so make sure your hands are free."

They held onto the rope during the crossing, and the cool current flowed chest high.

"I wonder what he would consider too high to cross," Joyia grumbled to Andy as she tossed her head in Juan's direction.

Andy laughed. "Good thing you aren't any shorter. You'd need scuba gear instead of hiking boots."

During a heart-pumping hike up steep grades, the Gran Sabana's grasses transformed to ferns. Andy wished he had time to take in their surroundings with more appreciation, but he drank in the beauty he could as it was. Rain was once more falling, making it impossible to set up their tents when they stopped for the night. Instead they set up camp in an abandoned shack to shelter from the downpour. They huddled under the shack's palm-thatched roof above straw flooring, surrounded by mud that was knee deep. Andy speculated that this would make a good pig farm, but that was the only complaint. They were making good time.

Rain beat down the entire night. The next morning the three hikers slipped in the mud and hay as they got their gear together and ate some protein bars for breakfast.

Andy stepped out of the dilapidated hut first. He eyed his surroundings, looking for a spot to relieve himself. Two things happened at the same moment. Andy lost his footing in the mud and landed on his butt, and a rifle shot rang out, followed by a chunk of earth exploding when the bullet hit it.

"Shit!" Andy yelled as he scrambled for some cover. Joyia came running out the door, and Andy screamed, "Get down, get down!"

Joyia dove behind a large boulder situated just outside the door. Another rifle crack shattered the morning as a bullet ricocheted off the boulder shielding Joyia.

"Juan, stay in the shack," Joyia commanded. She pulled out her 9 mm, knowing that it didn't have the distance needed to hit the individual shooting at them. Hell, she couldn't even see where the shot came from. She poked her head out, using the overgrowth to hide her movements. As her eyes scanned the surrounding area she caught sight of light reflecting off what must be the rifle's scope.

As she tried to figure out what the next step should be, the barrel of a rifle poked out from between the boards of the hovel and belched smoke as it returned a bullet in the direction of the glinting scope. The bullet sent a ripple through the leaves surrounding the unknown shooter, followed by a larger disturbance as the shooter moved out of position.

While the unknown gunman was too far away to make out any details, both Joyia and Juan saw the figure fleeing. Juan let off another shot for good measure. Andy was facing the shack, so he didn't see any of the activity, but he was reassured that all was good when Juan came out the door of the shack and no one tried to kill him.

"Damn drug runners," Juan cussed as he ambled out into the clearing.

Andy got up. His clothing was caked with mud.

"Are you all right?" Joyia asked.

Andy nodded and turned to Juan. "Is this normal? Should we expect this throughout the trip?"

"Never know, senor. It don't happen too often, though." He shrugged his shoulders but seemed unconcerned. It probably registered to him on the same level it registered to anyone driving a car that they might get hit by another car.

The group continued, though now both Andy and Joyia were more paranoid and acted more cautiously as they continued upward on the trail.

"Be careful where you place your hands during this final two-mile climb," Juan cautioned. "There are two poisonous snakes that call these rocks home—the coral and the deadly macagua. A hiker was bit last week and is still in the hospital. He is lucky. Most don't even make it to the hospital."

Andy and Joyia placed their hands wherever they could grab a grip while climbing the rain-slickened clay. Once again rain fell, mixing with their sweat as they passed through patches of dense jungle. At one point they scrambled on all fours while water cascaded from a cliff and beat down on their backs.

Exhausted and yet exhilarated, Andy felt alive as he shed his clothes, still muddy from the morning's close call, and jumped into a pool of cool water at the top of the summit. It was easy to see why this milieu inspired the setting for Sir Arthur Conan Doyle's *The Lost World*.

As Joyia looked around, her imagination started to create images from the bizarre rock formations. Juan pitched the tents on a good-sized ledge while Andy and Joyia climbed on the rocks and explored the caverns.

Crystals gleamed at random. This lost world was home to hundreds of rampant flora and fauna species.

That evening the group settled in to a dinner of macaroni mixed with carrots. They all agreed that dinner never tasted so good. A rare break in the clouds rejuvenated the bedraggled hikers. At Juan's urging, Joyia and Andy raced to the top of a mesa with hopes of catching a glimpse of sunset. Nightfall blanketed the campsite, but a break in the storm clouds allowed a full moon to light up their clearing. The break in the clouds, combined with the brightness of the full moon, allowed them a rare look over the massive Gran Sabana below. To the west, Mount Kukenan loomed.

They had no other confrontations with shooters on their two-day descent and greeted climbing trekkers they passed with encouragement. The climbers they passed assumed that they had come up from Santa Elena de Uairen as they had to in order to start the climb. Joyia was right. They blended in seamlessly. At one of the last river crossings, Andy stripped to his boxer shorts to cross the river.

"I'm not getting my last pair of pants totally soaked," he informed his curious companions. The water ended up being only shin deep, which caused Joyia to laugh so hard that tears started to flow down her cheeks. The day was overcast, providing them relief from the tropical heat, which Joyia took as a good omen for the rest of their trip.

The dirty, dusty threesome walked into Santa Elena de Uairen by late afternoon. Their appearance was not out of the ordinary, as the city was not only the jump-off point for tourists planning hikes into the Gran Sabana but also the returning point. There were many others who had just returned who were as dusty and muddy as they were. Established in 1923 by Venezuelan gold-hunter Lucas Fernández Peña, Santa Elena de Uairén sat near Venezuela's borders with Brazil and Guyana, about 870 miles by road from Caracas. It had an agreeable climate with mild temperatures all year round. It boasted a population of around thirty thousand people and was considered a small, safe, friendly community. The town itself was not particularly beautiful, but there were plenty of shops, restaurants, Internet cafés, telephone services, pharmacies, pool halls, and a few places where tourists could enjoy an evening beer.

The first priority was to get to the hotel where Juan had arranged for Elena to meet them before they left Brazil.

The hotel was big by Santa Elena standards, with clean, spacious rooms and bathroom areas, conveniently located away from the center of town but close enough to shops so that they could easily walk there if they wished to purchase anything. Although it could never measure up to the type of hotel that Andy normally liked to patronize, it was the one most popular with families traveling in from Brazil. Many Brazilians from Manaus and Boa Vista stayed at this hotel on their way to the coast. Elena and Juan had brought their family here several times, so Elena was familiar enough with the property to know which rooms were the best to book. There was a restaurant in the hotel, and although it was not gourmet, it would do for the short two nights they would be staying.

Elena had managed to get them two rooms right by the pool, which gave them some access to Wi-Fi in their rooms if they sat close to the window. At that point the three hikers were only concerned with a shower, food, and a bed.

As the rooms were reserved under Elena's name, there was no record of them being there, which provided some comfort to Andy. Although he felt his forged passport would pass muster with the Venezuelan authorities, he wasn't interested in testing it out too quickly.

Both Andy and Joyia let their backpacks drop to the floor the moment they entered their room. Andy sat on the chair closest to the door and peeled off his hiking boots. His feet were raw and blistered. A patchwork of moleskin was taped to various parts of his feet to protect the damaged flesh from further injury. Part of him wondered if he would have been better off wearing his Italian loafers. That thought made him turn to Joyia and say, "Remind me to call Koshka and arrange for a cleanup team to get my things out of the Aipana hotel. I doubt very much I will be going back that way."

Joyia only nodded in reply. Moving her lips would require too much effort from muscles pushed beyond their endurance. She plopped on the floor and commenced removing her boots and damp socks.

"I get the shower first," Andy declared, but he didn't make any effort to move.

"Can't we just shower together? I can't wait to wash the filth from my skin." Joyia also remained motionless.

Andy looked at her for a moment and relented. "Sounds good."

After a few minutes, he moved first, standing over Joyia and holding his hand out to help pull her up. She groaned but, with his help, achieved an upright position. With their arms around each other, they hobbled into the bathroom, where they removed their clothes before getting into the shower and allowing the cool water to run over them. They scrubbed themselves and each other, reaching those spots they couldn't reach on their own. After washing off the many layers of dirt, sweat, and mud, they dried off and stumbled into bed. Both were sleeping soundly within seconds of their heads touching the pillow.

Fifteen

Dusk had settled on Santa Elena de Uairén when Denise finally reached the town limits. She was furious at having missed the shot up in the mountain area, but she was more concerned at the moment with finding a place to stay and getting cleaned up. She was hungry and wanted to find someplace to eat where she could get a decent meal without going to too much trouble. Maybe a hotel with room service, if she could find one. After taking care of those immediate needs, she would start tracking Andy and Joyia.

She saw several hotels clustered along the main thoroughfare just after coming onto the street from where the trail had dumped her out. As she sized up the buildings for one that looked clean but cheap, she caught a glimpse of a section of a back bumper to a jeep. Denise couldn't be sure, so she walked toward the Sabana Hotel parking lot until she was close enough to reveal a larger portion of the vehicle. It was the same white Jeep Wagoneer that had dropped off Andy and his group at the trailhead several days ago.

She was willing to bet that the guide's partner had driven across the border and made arrangements for rooms for the hikers when they got into town. A quick look under the back bumper revealed that the tracking device was still intact, which meant that she would be able to track their movements to their destination. *Today must be my lucky day*, she thought. The sign at the entrance advertised vacant rooms, so she went into the lobby and got a room for herself. The desk clerk said that they did provide room service.

Denise decided she would shower, eat, call Peter, and then walk around the property to see if she could pinpoint what room her target was in. It was a large hotel but still small enough that she hoped her efforts would meet with success.

Denise felt better after her shower and a decent dinner. The worst part of the day was still ahead—calling Peter.

Peter's phone didn't even have the opportunity to complete the first ring before he answered and demanded the status of her work.

"I thought I had the perfect opportunity when crossing the Grand Sabana, but it didn't happen." She spoke almost nonchalantly, but inside she was still pissed that she had missed the shot.

"What the hell do you mean, it didn't happen? Where are you?" Peter shrieked into the phone. "You're supposed to be a professional. I paid you for being a professional. Where is the son of a bitch?"

Denise took a deep breath and tried to remain calm. "We are all in Santa Elena."

"Where is that?"

"Venezuela."

"Jesus Christ!" Peter ran his hands through his hair in frustration. "Could you not even keep him out of the country?"

"This will happen. Did I not get the State Department operatives kicked out? That had to slow them down. In fact, that's what has him running into Venezuela at this very moment, to get the coup back on track. I'll get this done."

"You aren't being paid to get State Department dullards thrown out of a country. You were contracted to eliminate one simple person. Just one. Is that too difficult for you to manage?"

"I will take care of it. I always complete my contracts."

"See that you do, or you can kiss your ass good-bye." With that, Peter hung up.

Denise sat for a moment, not moving, fuming. She fantasized shooting Peter in the head, up close and personal. Having the satisfaction of at least a brief instant of revenge, she turned her attention back to her task and headed out of her hotel room onto the grounds.

Denise did not have the same luck spotting them as she had with their jeep. She was afraid to sleep too long and wake up to find them gone. Although she still had the tracking device in her possession, it wouldn't set off an alarm to notify her if the Wagoneer moved. She had to find them.

She decided that she would sleep in two-hour intervals. The window to her room overlooked the parking lot, so she could check to see if the jeep was still there when she woke after each two-hour segment.

Denise followed her plan of waking and checking every two hours, but when the sun broke through the darkness, announcing a new day, the Wagoneer had not moved. Denise cleaned up and pulled a baggy, light hoodie over her head. It was big enough to hide the gun and holster she had on underneath. It was time to go hunting again. Maybe this time she'd spot someone from the group.

Andy was disoriented when he first woke. A sliver of bright sunlight broke through a small slit where the window curtains did not quite meet. It took him a moment of looking at his surroundings before the last twenty-four hours came flooding back into his mind. The hike into Venezuela had been an arduous journey, which included someone shooting at him—or at them, as Juan had insisted it was a drug smuggler warning them off.

Andy shook his head at the memory as he felt the warm body next to him move. Joyia stretched out like a large cat waking from her slumber. The movement was languid and arousing as Andy watched her come to life. He reached out to enjoy a little release for some pent-up physical frustration, only to get his hand smacked.

"Andy," Joyia admonished. "I am hungry. You have to feed me first. Do you think this body runs on air?" she asked as her hands made a gliding gesture down her body.

Andy groaned as he lay back into the bed.

Joyia reached over him and grabbed the phone. "I'm ordering room service. You want anything?"

"Eggs, bacon, toast, pancakes, coffee…" his voice trailed off as he stroked her bare back with his hand.

Her eyes opened in amazement at his list. "Gluttony is a sin."

"Your body is a sin."

Joyia laughed and pushed the buttons on the phone.

Through the hotel wall, they could hear Juan and his wife moving around. Their conversation was low, and Andy could not make out their words. Shortly thereafter, they heard the door to the room open and close as the couple left the room to go out. They were not scheduled to leave until tomorrow morning just before dawn to start the long drive to Caracas.

Another person also tracked their departure from the room. Denise caught sight of the couple as she ambled aimlessly around the hotel grounds. She did not see any sign of Andy and wondered if the two couples had split up at this point. Without any way of knowing what had happened and what plans had been made, Denise fell in step behind the two at a discreet distance.

It wasn't long before the Brazilians stopped at a streetside café to enjoy a leisurely breakfast. Denise had to be content with waiting for the two to finish to see if they were heading anywhere else—perhaps a rendezvous point with Andy and Joyia. If not, she would wait until they returned to their room and question them on what they knew of Andy's plan.

In the meantime, Andy and Joyia were enjoying a very well-prepared breakfast with plates loaded with food.

Their conversation was light until Joyia asked Andy if he knew the history of CLU. How did they become a partner of the CIA?

Andy was surprised. "I thought you would have known about that when you were brought onboard?"

"I know a little, but not much," Joyia responded.

"Well it's simple enough. After World War Two, the US was afraid that communists would infiltrate the European unions as they struggled to rebuild, and of course that would not be in the best interest of the US."

"I thought Russia was your ally in that war?"

"They were, but when the war was over, it became a pissing match between the two biggest dogs left on the block. Both wanted to be the only superpower, and their totally different political beliefs made them natural enemies. The Germans were gone, so without any other enemy in common, it was natural they would square off against each other. Communism in itself, the belief, was that the disciples of its principles were to spread it all over the world. Like the Islamic extremists do today."

Joyia nodded in encouragement, waiting for him to continue.

"So the powers that be in the government knew George Meany, head of the AFL. The AFL had not merged with the CIO at that time. Well, they knew old George was a passionate anticommunist, so they enlisted him to help out. So he did. After that, well, they formed an alliance that worked for both of them. I suppose there have been presidents and AFL-CIO leaders who wanted out, but the whole thing was designed to be outside of such individual disruption. Labor is the perfect way to get involved in other countries. We always get invited in by the working class, and because we aren't a government agency, we can operate without much oversight. Not many know we operate hand-in-hand with the US government. Because of that, we can also infiltrate groups like Occupy Wall

Street and control it in a way that won't cause much damage to our government."

"That is very clever," she said in admiration.

Andy turned to her. "What were you told?"

"Just that it was an organization that was funded by grants from the State Department to go in and help people establish democracies in their countries."

"Well, I guess that's a pretty simplistic explanation, but it'll do."

A couple of hours passed as Andy and Joyia ate and then indulged in satisfying their more carnal appetites. They soon heard Juan and Elena return to their room.

Joyia grabbed Andy's hand and pulled. "Let's take a shower."

Andy smiled and allowed himself to be pulled into the bathroom and under the hot water.

As Juan reached for the door to his and Elena's room, a voice softly spoke to Juan.

"Don't say anything, or I will kill her."

He turned to see another woman with her hand grasping his wife's hair and pointing a 9 mm with a silencer at her head. Juan's eyes quickly scanned the area and saw no one close enough to help. He thought quickly of Andy and Joyia next door but quickly discarded that when he saw the woman press the gun hard against his beloved's head.

He turned and unlocked the door, letting all three of them into the room. Denise used her foot to close the door behind her once she entered.

"Sit down," she ordered Juan, using her gun to indicate the chair. Juan could see the fear in his wife's eyes. She was terrified, so he did as he was told, hoping this crazy gringa would let them live. Juan was a great guide but a horrible fighter.

"Where are the two people you guided through the Sabana?" she asked, as she pushed Elena down on her knees.

"I don't know. We parted ways when we got into town," Juan responded, his voice trembling.

There was a small pop. Elena cried out, and Juan saw that Denise had shot his wife in the calf.

"No, please, senora, she knows nothing," Juan begged.

"Really? Then she truly is worthless." Denise fired again and Juan watched his wife's body go limp as she crumpled to the floor, a small hole above her ear.

Juan cried out in anger and pain as he charged Denise. "Fuck you, Puta!"

Denise fired again, this time shattering his knee. Juan found himself on the floor.

"One more time, where are they?"

Tears streamed out of Juan's eyes, both in pain and at his loss. "They are heading to Caracas. I know nothing else. Please, senora, I gave you what you wanted."

"Caracas is a big city," she said as she jerked his hair.

"I am just a guide." Juan did not know who this woman was, and he did not really know who the couple was that he had led across the Gran Sabana. He knew they had hired him to avoid a border stop, but nothing else. The couple he had guided could be smuggling drugs or something else he was better off not knowing about. They, on the other hand, knew that he had seven sons in Boa Vista. He could not risk the thought that they might be placed in danger if he were to reveal where Andy and Joyia were. After all, they might seek their revenge on his family if they thought he said anything.

"How very true," she said and then shot him in the back of the head.

She looked around the room and spotted their luggage. She quickly rifled through it and found nothing of interest. She pocketed the roll of American dollars she found as well as the Brazilian Reals. Having touched nothing in the room, there was nothing to wipe down. The whole situation had taken less than fifteen minutes. She made her way out the door, leaving nothing behind but two dead bodies.

Andy and Joyia dried off and, feeling well rested, decide to explore the hotel grounds and maybe even the town before they left the next morning.

As they walked out the door, Joyia turned to Andy. "We should see if Juan and Elena want to join us. They could take us to the more interesting spots. They must know the town well, with him being a guide in the Sabana."

Andy agreed, and they went next door and knocked. There was no answer.

"I thought I heard them come back before we got in the shower," Joyia said.

"I did, too." Andy went over to the window and tried to peer inside through the split between the curtains. He did not see either of them, but he did see their luggage on the bed. It appeared to have been disturbed.

Joyia looked at him questioningly. He shook his head.

"I could only see their luggage. It looked like someone had gone through it, but it could just be that they are messy."

"I have a bad feeling about this, Andy. Something is wrong."

Denise had not gone far when she heard Andy and Joyia coming out of their room. The dense foliage that the hotel had used to create a lush environment around the hotel provided the perfect cover for her to hide behind. She watched the pair stand outside the guide's room. Joyia knocked, and then Andy tried to peer through the window. The two were involved in a discussion again.

Denise was close enough, so, taking advantage of the cover the leafy plants provided, Denise pulled out her weapon and quickly fired without lining up her shot.

The wood doorframe next to Andy's head exploded as the bullet struck.

"Shit!" Andy threw all his weight against the door. It took two tries before the door gave, and they both fell into the room. Denise had managed to get another shot off, and it struck Andy in the shoulder.

He kicked the door shut as another bullet hit the wall in the room. They both were instantly cognizant of the two bodies in the room, but both were focused on defending their position. Calling the police was out of the question, especially now that their guide and his wife lay dead on the floor.

Joyia was digging into her purse as she asked Andy if he had been badly hit.

"No. It went through the flesh."

Joyia pulled two small pistols out of her purse. One would be worthless as it was a two-shot derringer meant for very close-up defense. The other was a small pistol whose accuracy at anything over twenty yards would also be questionable. Both were made for close contact.

"Hand me the pistol and then see if you can locate the keys to the Jeep," Andy instructed.

Joyia pushed the pistol toward him, staying low to the floor as she made her way to where Juan's body lay. Andy situated himself by the window as Joyia searched through Juan's pockets, looking for the keys. After a moment she held them up triumphantly.

Andy nodded. There weren't any other shots fired after the door to the room was closed, and Andy wasn't sure if the shooter was still there or had gotten out of town before the police or federales showed up.

The wait seemed to go on forever as they both huddled together. Joyia crawled to the bathroom and retrieved a wet rag to try to clean up Andy's shoulder and assess the damage. She pulled his shirt down and carefully dabbed at the blood around the edges of the wound. The shot was through and through, which was a relief. She wouldn't have to dig it out. She reached out from the floor and grabbed a pillow. She stripped off the pillowcase and, using the pocketknife that she always carried with her, shredded the pillowcase into strips. The bullet had hit a spot that made it awkward to wrap.

"I need tape," she said. Once more, staying close to the floor, she hustled over to the bags that belonged to Juan and Elena. She selected the backpack that Juan had carried through the Sabana, figuring that it probably had some sort of first-aid kit in it. She was rewarded with a compact but extensive kit in a waterproof case at the bottom of the pack. She scrambled back to Andy's side and, after applying a liberal amount of antiseptic, taped a thick gauze pad over the wound.

"Hurry," Andy urged as they heard sirens in the distance.

"Done," Joyia declared.

"We need to get our backpacks from the other room," Andy said.

"Let me go, since you're the target." Joyia went and cracked open the door to peer out. No shots were fired. She saw hotel staff running in different directions, but in general, there was no panic by the guests.

She turned back to Andy. "I think our shooter called the police on us. Maybe to flush us out."

Andy had a questioning look on his face. "What do you mean? I'm the target."

"Not now, Andy. Can't you see there are other problems more pressing."

"I think being a target for a crazed shooter is a pretty pressing problem."

Her look turned to one of exasperation. "Oh my God. This is not a crazed shooter. It's a contract hit."

Joyia darted out the door, and Andy listened for the sound of gunfire. Instead he heard the door to the other room open.

He waited a couple of minutes and then followed suit. As he helped Joyia gather their things and head out the door, he muttered, "You knew someone was trying to kill me, and you didn't think that was something I should know?"

Joyia huffed as she walked out the door without commenting. Andy followed, struggling to pull a hoodie over his head to cover the blood on his shirt and the wound in his shoulder. "Joyia, don't just walk away from me. I deserve an explanation."

The only explanation he got was a steady stream of curses in Portuguese, which continued as they entered the parking lot and headed toward the Jeep Wagoneer. As they were stowing their gear into the back of the Jeep, police cars skidded into the parking lot. The officers scrambled out of their patrol cars and paid no attention to the poor man being harangued by the woman in the parking lot.

Sixteen

Andy got into the passenger side of the Jeep, allowing Joyia to take over the duties. She knew the terrain better. She pulled out of the parking lot and quickly got them on the road to Caracas.

"Joyia," Andy snapped. "Who is trying to kill me, and why didn't you tell me?"

"*Madre de Dios*," Joyia exclaimed. "Don't you think you are overreacting just a bit?"

"Why no, Joyia, I don't think I'm overreacting. Excuse me for getting a little upset. I guess I just get a little nonplussed that someone is specifically trying to kill me." Andy paused a moment. "That guy in the mountains was probably trying to kill me, too!"

Joyia nodded. "Yes, I think so, too."

Andy's eyes grew wide as he continued to look at her.

"Don't look at me like that," she said. "It's not like I lied to you or something."

"Haven't you ever heard of lying by omission?" Andy was still incredulous that she knew someone was trying to kill him and never told him.

"No, I haven't. And that's a stupid saying anyway." Joyia had a stubborn set to her chin.

Andy slumped in his seat. The adrenalin was seeping out of his body, and his shoulder started to ache from the bullet wound. He rubbed his eyes. "Well, now that I know, can you fill me in on the details?"

"Are you still mad at me?" she asked.

"Yes, I am mad, but I will be less mad if I know why and how the hell this all happened!" Andy exploded.

"I don't want you to be mad at me."

Andy's look conveyed what he was feeling at that moment, disbelieving the conversation that was taking place. He took a deep breath and tried again.

"I won't be mad at you if you tell me everything."

She looked at him with candid suspicion. "Dane told me that someone was hired to kill you. A woman. He told me not to tell you because Koshka wanted you to focus and not lose sight of the mission. He's right, you know, Andy." She reached over and patted his knee. "You do overreact. You are very high-strung, and you would not have been able to concentrate." Joyia finished like she was talking to child.

"Well, gee, I admit that I might have been less focused on the mission and more focused on staying alive…"

"See," she interrupted. "This was a much better way then."

Andy stared at her look of self-satisfaction, believing he had just admitted she was right.

"This isn't over, Joyia. I'll be taking this up with Dane when I talk to him."

Joyia said nothing as she concentrated on the road.

It was a fourteen-hour drive to Caracas, give or take, and most people making the trip would stop overnight in Ciudad Bolivar. That was a part of their original plan, but with the murder of their guide and his wife and the revelation that there was someone trying to kill him, Andy decided they would drive straight through. They would take turns driving and stop for gas and food to eat on the road.

Andy took over for Joyia and assumed the driving responsibilities fairly early. It would be easier for her to maneuver the city roads in Caracas than him. She slept soundly as the pair barreled down the highway. Joyia woke up briefly, and her eyes glittered with tears. Andy looked over at her with concern.

"What's wrong, Joyia?"

"I was just thinking about Juan and his wife. It is so sad. They had children, and now they will be orphans."

"I will make sure Koshka sees that they are taken care of. I'm sorry they died, too."

They both went silent, and when Andy looked over at her a few minutes later, he could see that Joyia had drifted back to sleep. Andy pushed the speed limits as far as he was able. Joyia had made a call to Dane earlier, asking him to arrange for a room for them as they had no idea where Elena had booked them. Plus, as the rooms were booked under her name, they wouldn't be able to use them anyway. Joyia didn't relay to Dane everything that had transpired. She only gave him a quick rundown. They would all talk when they got to the hotel.

It took them a couple more hours than they had planned on to reach the hotel as it was located on the coast, on the north side of Caracas; but once they pulled in, Andy had no doubt that Dane was trying to kiss up to him prior to the call between the two of them tomorrow morning. He knew Dane would book at a Marriott as it was his favorite hotel chain, but his colleague really outdid himself with this one.

The Venezuela Marriott Hotel Playa Grande was located right on the beach in Catia La Mar. Andy sighed with pure pleasure when he spotted the portico complete with valet. He was back in his element.

As Joyia pulled the badly beaten Wagoneer up to the waiting valet, Andy stepped out of the vehicle and immediately questioned the valet on the availability of clothing stores.

The valet's English was excellent, and he informed Andy that there were several local places nearby and that the hotel would be happy to provide a shuttle—or, if Andy preferred, many of the best tailors would be happy to come to the hotel to display their wares to him in the room. If the senor would like, he could make arrangements with the concierge's desk.

Finally, Andy thought. *Civilization.* Andy truly was a dandy in every respect. In the world of foreign affairs, Andy was fonder of the James Bond image then that of the Navy SEAL. That was more Dane's forte.

The couple entered a beautiful, spacious lobby. Although the decor was contemporary, it spoke of money and class. They checked in and declined the assistance of a bellman. They didn't have much to carry. Arrangements were made for merchants from nearby clothing stores to visit the suite that Dane had so graciously provided.

He really is sucking up, Andy thought. The room itself was sumptuous, with a partial ocean view from a spacious balcony. The executive lounge was one floor up on the eleventh floor. Very convenient for Andy. It also had all the modern media features that Andy would need to carry out his business. The hotel's location was also a stroke of genius. It was close to the airport and also provided an escape route by water should an emergency arise. Hopefully, that wouldn't happen. It was also outside of the potential hotspots once the revolution began, although Andy had to admit that if the chaos started while they were inside the city proper, they would play hell getting back to the hotel. He noticed the areas they drove through to get there. Those areas spoke of poverty and hunger. They would ignite easily when fueled with revolt.

Seventeen

The next morning, Andy and Joyia connected with Dane. They had the phone on speaker so that they could both converse with Dane at the same time.

Andy kicked off the conversation with what was uppermost on his mind the minute he heard Dane's voice on the line. "Why in the hell wasn't I told that someone was down here trying to kill me?"

"Calm down, bro. I think you're overreacting a bit."

"If one more person tells me that I'm overreacting because I found out someone is trying to kill me—"

"All right, Andy," Dane interrupted. "We get it. Next time we'll tell you. Can we get down to the business at hand?"

"I want to know why someone is trying to kill me. What do you mean, next time?"

He could almost hear Dane's patience wearing thin through the phone speaker. "All right, Andy. Here's the story. It seems that the president's chief of staff has decided that our plan down here is not something that is good for his president's agenda. Since CLU operates outside of any political influence, it's not like the president or his chief of staff could stop it. So the little sycophant decided to go outside the box to stop this. They decided that if they took out the planner, then the rest would fall apart. That simple. Sorry we didn't tell you, but we just thought you wouldn't be able to concentrate. Joyia knew to be on the lookout."

"I got shot at twice!"

"You're alive!" Dane countered.

"I was hit in the shoulder!" Andy's voice went up several octaves.

"It was a through and through! Geez, slap a Band-Aid on it and call it good." Dane just couldn't comprehend why Andy was going on about this. Coming out of Special Forces and having done tours in Afghanistan as well as Iraq, this injury wouldn't have even merited a visit to the medic.

There was a moment of silence as the two men both dug in, preparing to defend their arguments further. By that point Joyia had gotten bored with whole discussion and stepped in. "Boys, boys, can we get on with what we're here to do? By the way, the hotel and the room are delightful. Thank you, Dane."

"You're welcome. Thank you for appreciating my efforts in making sure you're both comfortable." He then continued on with a different subject. "I'm sitting up here at the border, and my men are getting restless. I plan on moving into Maracaibo within the week. I have people in Valencia, Caracas, Petare, Barcelona, San Cristobal, Maturin, and Ciudad Bolivar. They've been deployed in groups of six to nine, depending on the neighborhoods. We have a little under a hundred people in the cities and a couple of groups roving through the more rural areas. We're ready to go."

In the back of his mind, Andy registered that the men whom Dane would soon be setting loose on Venezuela were men who would take their payment in the form of goods that they looted from the stores that had the misfortune of being in the midst of the rioting.

"OK, let me retrace the steps of our expelled diplomats and see where we are," he said. "I need to reconnect with Francisco and Marco. Joyia and I need to get the university students organized. We need to get this rocking and rolling. Oil prices have dropped, and the government here is under a financial strain that their good buddies the Ruskies can't help them with, having to deal with their own crippled economy. Crime is rampant. The people's lot in life has not improved. Let's make sure we're ready to capitalize on the window of opportunity while it's open. We don't know how much longer it'll be open."

"Andy, I think that I could do a lot more in the ghettos around the city than on the campuses. Maybe I can get Francisco to help me with that," Joyia said.

"Make sure that you don't go into the barrios without some good bodyguards. That's not the place to be alone," Dane warned.

"I will, but I'm also capable of defending myself. I am very familiar with Brazilian jujitsu," Joyia replied. Joyia had attended the Gracie family jujitsu academy in Sao Paulo. Brazilian jujitsu was adapted from Japanese jujitsu into its contemporary form by the Gracie family. It was a ground fighting system that included submissions such as chokes, arm locks, and foot locks. With proper technique, a smaller, weaker person could success-fully defend him- or herself against a larger, stronger opponent. "Not to mention my familiarity with handguns," she added.

"OK, let me reach out to everyone, get us on track. Dane, I'll try to give you a heads-up on this, but it may break quickly, so just be ready."

"We'll be ready," Dane affirmed.

"All right, let's get this done, ladies and gents."

Eighteen

The next couple of days were spent getting appropriate clothing so that they could mingle on campuses, in town meetings, and so Joyia could go into the barrios. Andy also wanted to get his plan nailed down.

He looked over what he had originally designed and what now had to be modified. Through the Catholic and other private universities, he could offer up classes and assistance in applying for visas as a reason to hold group meetings. He would definitely need Marco for that kind of help.

Joyia walked over to the desk where he was working in the suite. Andy looked up when he felt her hand rest on his shoulder.

"I'm heading down to the lobby to meet Francisco. We're going to head into the ghettos."

She was dressed in some fashionably torn jeans that fitted her well. Nike knockoffs encased her feet. A T-shirt with some modern geometric patterns topped off the ensemble, and she had a light jacket draped over her arms.

He stared pointedly at her Nike knockoffs.

"I want to fit in. I can't be bopping through the barrios in name-brand clothing. It's hard to relate to people there when your shoes cost more than what they make in a month."

Andy just grunted and didn't reply.

"Do you want me to close the door to the balcony before I leave?" Joyia asked.

"No, I like to hear the ocean. It helps me think." Andy turned his body to face her. "Joyia, be careful."

She leaned over and gave him a kiss on the cheek. "I will, my handsome man. I will try to be back in time to order room service for dinner."

He gave her a smile.

"Are you staying in?" she asked.

"Yes. Marco is meeting me here today, and then we'll make plans for the future meetings at the campuses."

"Well, you boys have fun."

Francisco was waiting in the lobby for her when she stepped off the elevator. He had on a loose-fitting, long-sleeved white shirt and a pair of faded jeans. He held out his hands as she approached.

"Francisco." She took his hands and pecked him on the cheek. They were a handsome couple and drew many admiring looks as they walked out of the hotel. *It is too bad he is gay*, Joyia thought. He would have made an excellent escort to the many galas and parties that Joyia found herself going to as well as someone whose looks would make it a pleasure to bed.

Francisco had a sporty little car. It was not a high-end car, but for those with a middle-class salary, it was a popular selection.

The mountains and hillsides that surrounded Caracas were covered in shantytowns known as barrios. The first stop was not far from the hotel where they were staying. However, it took a long time to get there because traffic was incredibly bad. Because gas was priced at only twenty cents a gallon, driving was encouraged at the expense of public transportation.

Francisco drove his car into a secured parking garage. They would walk the rest of the way in. The combination of incredible traffic and aged cars produced the worst pollution that Joyia had encountered in a long time. The smell of fuel and oil tainted the air she breathed. Most buildings they walked past seem to be abandoned monuments to a more prosperous past, as people navigated through refuse and merchant stalls selling every conceivable fake piece of rubbish from China.

"Tell me about this barrio we are going to, Francisco," Joyia prodded.

"Even the *policia* don't go in into the barrios. Cars can't fit in through the alleys, which is why we parked the car and will be on foot the rest of the time. When the policia do venture in, they ride on motorcycles, steering with one hand and shooting their guns with the other. Usually there is a second man who sits behind the guy driving the motorcycle. He has his back to the first policeman and fires from the back. But the policia or federales do not go there unless they are chasing a serial killer or someone as bad. The people who live here will shoot at the police. I go into some of the barrios, but not all. In many of them you walk through the streets, and people smoke crack out in the open with their guns next to them."

"So I'd get robbed if I went there alone," Joyia said.

"You'd get killed." Francisco looked her up and down quickly. "Probably raped first. Most of the time in this city, the policia are a part of the crimes. They see people being robbed and turn the other way for a cut of the stolen money. Most of the two thousand murders per year that happen here, happen in the barrios. These people, they were not always like this. Most are people from the countryside who came looking for a chance, a job during the city's prosperous times. Some barrios are not as dangerous and have a strong sense of community, one of which we are heading to right now. But they generally are not a place you want to be in. Nor will I take you to those barrios."

Francisco took a deep breath and continued his monologue. "In Caracas it's impossible not to see the huge disparity in living conditions. I know that what these men from the US are here to do will cause bloodshed, and people will lose what little they have when the true revolt starts. People will cradle their children as life leaves their bodies. I know that you come here to push in a government that the US would prefer to deal with—a political system that is more Americanized, to make this country a puppet of the American government. This I know. But if that's what it takes to change what you're about to see, then let the revolution begin. I don't care what the methods are or the reason. At some point, the people are so broken, the system of government oppression—of communism enforced by the boot of a soldier—is so bad that only extreme measures can break its hold on the people."

He took another deep, emotional breath and turned to her. "I would rather be the puppet of a benevolent giant than the punching bag of a petty dictator."

His emotional statement surprised Joyia. She had become so cynical that she assumed everyone was in it for their own enrichment.

"You're a good man, Francisco," she said softly. "Let's see if we can free these people from the chains of their barrios."

The barrios were home to those who had most loyally supported the late Hugo Chavez, yet they never saw the reward of a better life that Chavez promised would come from the government taking control of many of the businesses and redistributing the wealth.

As they walked through the narrow alleys littered with filth and refuse, people smiled. They were friendly for the most part. Some had set up little stands from which they sold over-ripened fruit and vegetables to their neighbors. Colorful paintings decorated the sides of building, giving a whole new meaning to the term "graffiti artist." Joyia felt eyes peeking through threadbare fabric in the windows, watching them. She smiled in greeting to those who watched them from the street.

Francisco led her into a building that was two stories high but unbelievably narrow. He tapped on the flimsy piece of plywood that acted as a door into the home.

They heard movement inside. An older woman opened the door and invited them in. She invited them to sit on two rickety chairs. As they balanced themselves on their precarious perches, a man walked into the room. He looked so very tired, his posture bent, but when Joyia's eyes met his, she saw a fire still burning there.

She was introduced to the man, and the woman offered her food and drink. She declined the offer, having been warned by Francisco that they would probably offer them the only food they had.

After pleasantries were exchanged, the man spoke. "When I was a younger man, the Yankees came here and tried to remove President Chavez. I believed in Chavez and fought in the streets to drive the Yankees out. He promised that the hunger would end. He said that once we pried the gold from the fingers of the very rich, we would all have plenty. Our children would have better lives and schooling. It was all a lie. Now President Gomez tells us that poverty causes crime. So why hasn't crime fallen? Because in Venezuela, poverty has not fallen. It's a fucking lie. We know better! We've seen the same people here in the barrios for twenty years! I weep for my country. But poverty—and cheap rhetoric—is what these politicians use to control us!"

The man held a position of respect in this barrio community, and because of that, he was able to communicate with others who held the same station in other barrios that surrounded Caracas. But there were some barrios that even he could not work within. Those barrios were too far gone. But they did not need all the barrios, just those who actually cared which government controlled their lives.

After they talked, the old man led them out into the barrio and showed them his community. Wherever he went, he was greeted with smiles and signs of respect.

At one point he stopped and asked Joyia, "How old do you think I am?"

Joyia stumbled over an answer, not wanting to insult the man with an incorrect guess.

As her discomfort was apparent, the man smiled and said, "I am forty-five years old. This life," he continued as his hands swept over the view of the hills the barrios were built on, "it takes much from a man."

As they walked through the depressing area, built by poverty and broken dreams, the man introduced her to the inhabitants of the clustered shanties.

In the distance the sound of a gunshot echoed through the community. But no one even twitched. The sound that should have registered fear among the residents had become too commonplace for them to react to.

While Joyia and Francisco met with those who occupied the various barrios that ringed Caracas, Andy and Marco were meeting with those from a more comfortable background.

Andy sat down with the university students, professors, and others attached to this social circle. With their input the blueprint for the Venezuelan revolt began to come to life. Like the poor, they, too, had found themselves increasingly victimized by a useless government under a petty dictator. Under the assumed name on the Canadian passport Joyia had gotten him in Boa Vista prior to their crossing the border, Andy spent time meeting with students of the universities under the pretext of assisting them in getting visas. Andy had the kind of congenial persona that lent itself to sharing with them tales of his youth, when he had often faced off against police during his own days as a student demonstrator. Andy made sure that the students he made contact with were ones who had been offered training and financing to create youth groups that would generate the violence needed to overthrow the government.

This was not a new model that Andy had invented. Those who had come before him decades ago had designed it. These centers were created and established around the globe in various countries. The students Andy met with had been selected and trained through CLU's outreach centers in advance of plan action, as well as others who came before them and were now working in media, elected to government offices, or operating businesses among the populace. This network could be counted on to act when the time came. Those who went through the outreach center were schooled in community organizing and had been actively doing so with those they worked and lived among. The outreach center kept track of these community organizers and the neighborhood groups they established, as well as the numbers of people they recruited through those groups.

Those numbers, as well as political-climate reports, were constantly being fed back to Washington through CLU. This action would have only been put into motion if the numbers were strong and the climate ripe for such brash action. As these centers had been operating under one guise or another for decades, the number of leaders and groups that could be counted on was high.

An important component of the plan was to present the students as a cohesive movement. This was not as challenging as it might seem. Venezuela's university system was notoriously exclusionary, and this applied both to private universities like the UCAB and selective public universities like the Universidad Central de Venezuela (UCV). In most of these institutions, which embodied the affluent historical Brahmans of Venezuelan society, they had substantial power, controlling most of the sanctioned student unions and political organizations.

Caracas alone boasted twenty thousand students, and these demonstrations would have to mobilize more than fifty thousand in order to gain serious attention from the outside world. At the same time that these mobilizations in the wealthy east of Caracas occurred, the youth huddling in the sprawling barrios that housed half of the city's population would also have to rise up. This was a critical piece of the plan. In 2002, it was the poor who had restored Chavez to power after an attempted coup. Whoever was the lead on that revolt had obviously not thought it through—or did a piss-poor job of recruiting out of the barrios. That was a mistake that had been corrected this time.

CLU's arm that had been operating in Venezuela since 1997, even if covertly at times, had encouraged and nurtured outreach between the two classes of university students for several years now. After all, the poor and the middle class would always outnumber the rich. Any revolt that did not embrace the working-class university students would certainly put a damper on Andy's plans. It was a classic strategy of common-interest goals that bind people from diverse backgrounds.

Of course, in this case, a common interest had to be created, but no matter. Andy was certainly experienced in creating the illusion of government oppression among all the youth of Venezuela. Of course, it actually wasn't as much of an illusion as it was the reality. Furthermore, the more affluent the students, the more put-upon they felt by even the most minor controls. After all, they were the ones with no limits placed on them at all by their families. And although they did not see themselves in the same social circle as those students in the government schools, it was in the DNA of all youth to rebel and associate with those whom their parents would deem unacceptable.

Andy smiled. Yes, his time with Occupy Wall Street certainly gave him a different angle for approaching certain problems. Along with the new knowledge of how to create a movement of people from diverse backgrounds, Andy had learned that black-blocking was an impressively effective tool in motivating people to break the law. A black bloc was a tactic for protests and marches in which individuals wear black clothing and ski masks or other face-concealing items. The clothing was used to conceal marchers' identities and hamper criminal prosecution by making it difficult to distinguish between participants. It served a dual purpose by protecting the protesters' faces and eyes from pepper spray and the like, which law enforcement often used to daze activists. The tactic allowed the group to appear as one large, unified mass, and thus it promoted solidarity. People often were braver and more likely to take chances if they felt they were anonymous. It was that created illusion of security that often allowed the protest marches to escalate into violence.

It would now be used in Venezuela. Shipments of Guy Fawkes masks had been brought in through Marco's connection and now resided in the storage rooms of universities and basements of churches. Andy loved orchestrated mayhem. The unchoreographed chaos surrounded and hid the carefully designed core.

Over the next month, meetings were held with students, farmers, and people in the barrios, with political activists leading them. Each group went over and over what would happen, how it would happen, and their part in it.

At the end of the last day, Andy felt tired and energized all at the same time. They were way ahead of where he had originally thought they were. He needed to see where the barrios stood. He hoped Joyia would have good news for him tonight. Both he and Marco were talked out as they climbed into Marco's car. The road back to the hotel was in silence, but it was a contented silence, born from the satisfaction of knowing that after years of indoctrination, the trouble and money spent would finally bear fruit. This grand plan had been in development ever since the first failed coup.

Andy got to the room to find Joyia reclining on the couch with a glass of wine, reading over her notes from the day. She looked up as Andy entered the room.

"How was your day?" she asked.

"Very enlightening." Andy turned to her and asked, "The barrios?"

"Just light the match."

"What have we got?" Andy asked, referring to the ability to communicate to the people who occupied Venezuela's poorest neighborhoods.

"Francisco's people have run cables to designated spots or central squares within the barrios and placed large screens there. He told the government that it was a charitable work by his unions to give the poor access to television. Over the past year, he has broadcast soccer games to those living there. The federales are no longer suspicious of the intentions of the unions. We can broadcast whatever you need us to."

Andy was more than pleased; he was ecstatic. The adrenalin started coursing through his veins in anticipation of the upcoming events. The need to make right what had failed many years ago would soon be fulfilled.

"Let's mobilize all the kids. We need to also alert our section leaders in the ghettos and the farmers' coalition. Having such a bad harvest this year really helped us with getting them to rally to the opposition's cause. We have a strategy as an organization right here." He tapped his notebook. "Let's activate the kids from the public universities first. We can avoid the government press puppets from labeling it as spoiled rich kids having a temper tantrum in the streets. Once the public students go, we can summon the students from the Catholic and private universities to march in support. I doubt the politicians will intervene, so that will leave it to the kids to create the upheaval in their natural environment. We'll give them support—stick them in trucks if we have any—so that this can spread to surrounding areas. What do you think?"

"The only thing that can hurt us in this situation is if something extraordinary happens," Joyia replied. "Do you think we'll have to preplan the deaths of a couple of students during a street protest to bring the condemnation of the world on the greasy *bastardo's* head?" Joyia asked in a tone that sounded like she was asking Andy if he wanted cream in his coffee.

Andy didn't even look up from the playbook he was sketching out. "Hope not. Kind of hoping that the Venezuelan police or military will take care of that for us. Are we prepared, just in case?"

"Si," she responded. "Dane has people in place with the correct uniforms and balaclavas for the face, as well as helmets. Had to make a trade with a Columbian drug dealer for the right guns. But now we are bueno. Ballistics will show it comes from the rifle of the policia or the military." Joyia's face showed no emotion as she spoke—and it wouldn't, because she had no emotion. It was a practical matter in her eyes.

Andy nodded absentmindedly as he stared at the flowchart he had created of his key people. "Just make sure that if our 'soldiers' have to kick things off, there is a news camera around—or, better yet, someone filming with a smartphone. Can't trust the government media, and I want this to reach every end of the globe."

Joyia made a huffing noise. "As often as these *Chavista* pricks have created fiction from facts, I will make sure that each of our boys has someone with a video camera nearby at all key points of intended violence."

"What is our ability to broadcast into the rural areas?"

"Spotty, but we'll have enough area covered that the rest will just spill over. Very similar to what you probably had in Tunisia."

Andy nodded. He was ticking off a mental checklist, thinking of where they were and where they needed to be and whether they were in position to kick this off.

He picked up his phone and called Dane. "I think we're ready," he stated as soon as Dane answered.

"You took your bloody time getting there. What's wrong? You didn't have the right wardrobe?" Dane needled him. "I'm curious, what is the appropriate fashion statement to make at a coup?"

"Why would it matter to you? You still think the mullet is a viable haircut," Andy retorted.

"I'm bald, shit-for-brains," Dane shot back.

"Oh yeah, my bad. You think Buddha is the new sex symbol," Andy cracked.

There was a moment of silence as Dane mulled over whether he should continue the personal slams or get down to business. Ultimately he decided to get down to business.

"I'm more than ready. The natives are getting restless in my case. The pay and lodgings are OK, but they're anxious for the party to start. The promise of being able to loot and steal is more appealing to them than the stipend we're throwing at them. We wait much longer, they will migrate back into the Narco trade to start making some real money."

"Good. I need to make one more call. Let's see. Today is Friday. Government will be closed Saturday and Sunday. Let's plan on Monday. Get your guys on notice," Andy directed.

"Done," Dane responded, and Andy heard a click, indicating that Dane had hung up.

The next call Andy made was to Koshka. She answered on the first ring.

"Tell me you have good news for me," she ordered.

"OK, I have good news for you," Andy replied.

There was a moment of silence as Andy could visualize Koshka pursing her lips at his glibness.

"Don't push me, Andrew," Koshka's voice came back, soft but strong.

"Oh, come on now, Koshka. Certainly I'm entitled to a push or two. After all, no one thought I was entitled to know someone was trying to kill me."

"Please, Andy. I already talked to Dane. Don't start crying over this again."

"I was shot, Koshka."

"Dane said it was a scratch."

"Dane wasn't the one who got shot!"

"OK, fine, you got shot; I'm sorry. Feel better now?" Patience was not one of Koshka's stronger suits.

"I'd feel better if the shooter had been shot. Maybe killed would be good."

"Yes, yes, Andy, we're working on it. Please tell me you didn't call me just to talk about drivel?"

Andy would have laughed at her pained tone if it weren't for the fact that she actually didn't tell him someone was trying to kill him. Something like that could really ruin a man's day.

"We're ready to go. Target day is Monday. Just waiting for you to say go," he offered.

The silence in itself was deafening. Andy knew that once Koshka gave the word, it would be a go, but it also meant that she would bear the sole responsibility if it failed. That's a heavy load to carry when you are talking about overthrowing governments and reshaping the world order. It would mean that, for all the bickering back and forth, she was placing a whole lot of trust in him.

"Go," she said and then hung up the phone.

Andy had turned his back to Joyia as he talked. He now turned his head back toward her and nodded. She returned the nod.

Nineteen

The initial efforts of the students appeared peaceful and democratic that following Monday. They wore casual clothing and were organized in their procession as they marched down one street and then turned onto another, which ultimately would lead them down a blind alley. This alley ended at the National Assembly and revealed with absolute clarity to all those who watched the rightness within the "unity" of the student movement.

The students continued on into the National Assembly. Quietly they chanted, "We are anonymous. We are legion. We do not forget. We do not forgive. We are coming."

They repeated the verse quietly over and over as they filed into the Assembly. The students numbered in the hundreds. It was early Monday morning, and although the doors to the building were open, the Assembly was not in session. In the office that lined the corridors off the main assembly floor sat elected and appointed officials who soon heard the commotion and made their way to the main floor.

Some students chained themselves to pillars or desks that had been bolted to the floors. By the time the last student filed through the door, the room was filled to capacity. They had taken over the National Assembly and would occupy it. This peaceful action would trigger a response from the military or police.

However, police would be careful not to use violence this early. They would surround the Assembly and try to prevent anyone else from entering. Among the students within the Assembly, many would take photos and videos from their smartphones and upload them to YouTube and Facebook, as well as other mass Internet information outlets. Photos would be sent to news outlets and journalists. They needed the world's eyes upon them. Most importantly, though, they needed their countrymen to see what they were doing. In a symbolic way that only their fellow countrymen would understand, it was a call to arms.

The first speaker to the podium was Michelle Guevara, a Partido Bandera Roja (BR) student leader and economics scholar from the government-sponsored Bolivarian University (UBV). In the 1970s and up until the 1990s, the BR was engaged in guerrilla warfare against the government. A young Hugo Chavez's first assignment in the army was as commander of a communications platoon attached to a counterinsurgency force—the Manuel Cedeño Mountain Infantry Battalion, headquartered in Barinas and Cumaná. In 1976, under the presidency of Carlos Andres Perez, it was tasked with suppressing the guerrilla insurgency staged by the party.

After the electoral victory of Hugo Chavez in 1998, the party started aligning itself with the right wing and social democratic opponents of Chavez, labeling him as a social fascist.

Andy had written Michelle's speech himself. He wanted her to kick off the encounter because she was from the barrio and was the antithesis of her more affluent comrades. She would wear a red shirt, symbolizing the Chavista supporters. Her speech, while well crafted, contained no arguments, only vague promises of the continued struggle for Venezuelans and, somewhat unexpectedly, a progression of national reconciliation. Halfway through, as she spoke of reconciliation, she removed her red Chavista shirt to reveal the white and blue, symbolizing the revolution. At the end of her speech, Guevara shouted with passion: "I dream of a nation in which we are not defined by the color of our shirts. Where we can be treated well by our government without having to wear a uniform of political correctness."

Other revolutionary student leaders in the chamber started removing their T-shirts, revealing a variety of pro-freedom messages. Cheers echoed through the halls. The toadies of the Gomez government went scrambling back to their offices and quickly dialed their superiors and well-placed party officials.

Her fervent speech was captured on video and in photos. Within minutes people around the world were seeing it. Those closer to home in the barrios had their regular sports programing interrupted as her speech was telecast live through the cable that had been laid with this express purpose in mind.

The people in the barrios crowded around the screens that had been placed within their poverty-stricken communities. They cheered the words of this woman who had risen from their ranks to deliver a message to the rest of the country. Michelle spoke of freedom from their despair; she spoke of throwing off this yoke of oppression.

She then invited those students who supported the Chavismo party and President Gomez to come to the National Assembly building. She invited students who supported the current government to participate in a debate with this group of students identifying with the revolution.

Whereas in the past, Chavista students had continuously emphasized their openness to debate the revolution-supporting students, the structure of the proposed debate threatened to fracture their meticulously constructed image as the sole representatives of the Venezuelan student population.

In other words, in the past they had been able to control the environment of the debate so that the opposition students appeared to be a small minority of extremists while they represented the majority. This time the truth would be apparent to those who watched around the world. This idea that the Chavista supporters were the majority was the fallacy that Andy's plan would completely blow out of the water. This was clearly a debate that the Chavista students couldn't accept. This was what Andy hoped would ignite the powder keg of revolt.

The revolutionary students began to withdraw from the Assembly. They marched, shouting their demands for freedom of expression as they withdrew from the city and made their way toward the outer neighborhoods. As they left they shouted at the top of their lungs, "*Libertad de prensa*" (press freedom) and "*Libertad de empresa*" (freedom of private businesses).

At this point they were joined by large groups of students of the UCV, which was a "free to all" government-sponsored university, led by a popular representative in the Venezuelan congress.

The UCV had for decades been a bastion of the poor and the left-wing thinking, but free education did little when there were no jobs and stores couldn't even put toilet paper on the shelves. And, of course, the communist organization, the Bandera Roja (Red Flag), was acting like the military arm of the insurgent students. No sooner had the group from UCV merged with the original student protesters than they were enveloped by a massive show of participation from students at USB (Universidad Simon Bolivar), another state-owned and state-managed free education center. Along with the students of the universities, there was also participation from the technical schools (i.e., community colleges). This was shaping up into a first-class revolution.

The two groups—the revolutionary students and the Chavista students—came together outside the National Assembly. Some of Dane's agitators made sure to grab the free red shirts that were available to the Chavistas. The red T-shirts were far more than a safety strategy for his men tucked into the Chavista crowd. They were an integral part of a professionally designed media strategy. Make no mistake about it, one way or the other, the first acts of violence would be launched by the Chavistas.

Dane was just hoping that they had enough ambition to start themselves, but if all else failed...

The two sides engaged in a shouting match that quickly escalated into violence. It was hard to say which side threw the first punch or whether it was the police or the students who fired the first shot.

It was hard to really pinpoint what action would set off a full-fledged rebellion. In Tunisia it was a burning man. Who knew what would be the last straw in Venezuela? Perhaps it would be this street brawl between opposing student factions. But history had taught all those who made rebellion a career choice that it was often the simplest and most inconsequential happening that would spark the riots.

Dane had some strategically placed paid agitators from Colombia, Brazil, and Bolivia who were encouraging more violent action by both sides, cheering the student mob on like spectators at an Ultimate Fighting Championship. Dane was good at coordinating his foot soldiers to interact and become integrated with the mob. All the Chavistas were decked out in red shirts to publicize their allegiance to the Venezuelan socialist government, chanting "Education first to the children of the worker, education second to the children of the bourgeoisie" and "The people have spoken, and they are right."

It was class warfare escalated to its highest fervor. One could only stoke the embers of class warfare so long before the two sides hated each other enough to kill. It had been that way throughout history. The Bolshevik Revolution, the French Revolution, and the Spanish Civil War all started with the seeds of class warfare. Anyone who planted those seeds in a population planted the seeds of the eventual downfall of a country.

The Venezuelan police and military started wading into the crowd and using their billy clubs to break up the mob. When they reached the Venezuelan representative who led the UVC students, they promptly arrested him under the charge of sedition. At this point both the revolutionary students and the Chavistas retreated, but neither side had surrendered.

Twenty

Denise strode through the hotel grounds. They were quite beautiful. It was a definite step up from the last hotel. It had taken Denise way too long to locate Andy's new digs, but eventually she got close enough to the tracker that was still attached to the jeep that had carried Andy and Joyia from Santa Elena to Caracas, pinged to the homing devise Denise had with her.

In the process of trying to locate him, Denise was sure that she had, at the very least, cruised 80 percent of the high-end hotels in Caracas. She had started with those, knowing Andy's penchant for luxury. Habits can leave one vulnerable. It was not a mistake Denise would make. She strolled casually, like a tourist enjoying the comforts that a certain amount of wealth brought, which those who stayed at this particular Marriott obviously had. Her mind played with different scenarios regarding how to take out her target. She had missed him twice now, so either the third time was the charm or she would strike out. She had heard about the protest that had occurred earlier outside the National Assembly. She was not sure if Andy's death would stop what had already been started, but she was sure that it would stop him from ever inciting the population of another country to overthrow their government. Andy had not left his room in two days, which she took to mean that he was carefully orchestrating his people during the most vulnerable part of any revolt—the beginning.

In the beginning stages, any number of things could destroy the movement. Maybe that meant she still had time. Either way, she needed a plan to get to him. Her only option would be room service. Although she had checked, and he had not ordered anything in the past twenty-four hours, she was sure she had a way to get him to open the door. And if he didn't open the door, well, she had a way of dealing with that, too.

Denise had spent several days doing recon. She now knew Andy's room number and had a room on the same floor. The truth was that Andy and Joyia were sloppy in protecting themselves from someone tracking them. Andy was predictable in his hotel choices, and Joyia was too flamboyant in her comings and goings from the hotel. It took the challenge out of the whole assignment, but she got paid no matter how easy the target made it for her.

Denise breezed into the employee locker room like she belonged there, and no one questioned the truth of it. She had pocketed a name tag from a waitress earlier with the old bump and grab move she had learned at the CIA. In a gym bag, she had clothing that matched the food and beverage uniforms worn by the hotel wait staff. They had not been difficult to duplicate. Armed with pictures she had taken, her first stop had been a secondhand store near the hotel, where she scored a shirt embroidered with the Marriott logo. The black pants and shoes were generic in their style, and she easily found those at a regular clothing store.

She padded her body around the hips to change its contour and threw in a blond dye job that left her dark roots exposed. A pair of heavy, black-framed glasses completed the transformation.

Down in the kitchen area, Denise grabbed a black apron from the shelf and then waited. She did not have to wait long before the strident voice of a prima donna chef demanded her attention. A room-service cart was sitting there with a food order on it. With the food was a bottle of champagne and a carafe of orange juice. Someone in the hotel was planning on indulging in mimosas this fine afternoon.

"You, lazy shit!" the chef cursed her. "Take this to the room before the food gets cold."

Denise grabbed the cart and pushed it through the door that led to the service elevator. She did not know which room it was supposed to go to, but she did know what room she was taking it to.

Using room service to assassinate someone had to be the oldest cliché in the book. In fact, it was often used in the movies, but there was a reason it had become a cliché. It worked. Denise had the service elevator to herself, and she used the time to put everything together in a way that would allow her to carry out her job in an efficient manner.

The ding of the elevator told her she had arrived at the right floor. She took one last look to assure herself that nothing would indicate to a passerby that she was delivering more than food before she pushed the room-service cart out of the elevator and toward Andy's room. Joyia had left that morning and had not returned yet, so Denise knew that Andy was alone. What she didn't know was how long that situation would remain unchanged. So she had to act quickly.

Arriving at his door, she knocked sharply and was rewarded by hearing movement within the room. Like most people who stayed in a hotel, when someone knocked on the door, the first thing the room's occupant did was walk to the door and look out the peephole. Andy was no different. He took in the pudgy blonde as he placed his eye at the peephole.

"I didn't order any room service." Andy's voice carried through the hollow door, alerting Denise to the fact that he was standing directly in front of the door. Her hand, hidden from Andy's view by a small stack of covered plates, twisted slightly as she picked up the pistol she had placed at her fingertips earlier. She fired right through the door. Two quick shots, and she was rewarded with a thud as his body hit the floor. She came around the cart with the intent of getting into the room and delivering a double tap to the head to make sure her contract had been completed.

At that moment, the guest elevator opened, revealing a group of laughing young couples. They made their way to the door right next to Andy's room. They banged on the door, encouraging a friend within to open it and join them. Denise could not make out the response, but it was obvious that the room's occupant was not coming out and that the group outside the door was not going to give up easily. Denise had no choice but to retreat to the service elevator with the room-service cart, the sounds of giggling and cajoling grating on her ears every step of the way.

Once in the elevator, Denise selected a button for a couple of floors down and quickly stripped off her disguise as the elevator descended. Once out of the elevator, she took the steps back up to the floor where her room was located. Slipping into her room unseen, she started the process of transforming her look, toning down the brassy blond hair, touching up the roots, shedding the glasses, and popping in green contacts. She removed the padding from her hips and completed her new look by wrapping her breasts with an ace bandage to flatten her chest. The pudgy, buxom bleached blonde was now a willowy, flat-chested, golden blonde.

Down the hall and around the corner from where Denise was going through her metamorphosis, Andy lay motionless on the floor of his room.

With her new look, Denise made her way to the beach by the hotel. It would be the perfect place for her to make her call to Peter. It would be difficult for anyone to overhear the discussion.

"It's done," she said, before Peter could say a word.

"Are you sure?"

"No Peter, I'm not. I just thought it would sound good when you answered the phone to say that. Kinda like they do in the movies at that one dramatic point," she fired back.

"No need to get bitchy. I'll have the money wired to your account immediately. What is happening there? Does it look like he had enough time to set things in motion?"

"Peter, their training centers have been here forever. I don't know how close things are. That wasn't my priority. I'm sure they're close to where they want to be. They have had their hand in the mix with the revolutionaries since Chavez."

"I heard Dane was in Colombia. Have you seen him?"

"Again, not my priority—unless you wish to add him to the contract for an additional fee. However, Columbia would be a good place if one wanted to get one's hands on some soldiers of the independent or drug cartel variety. Hell, with the historic relationship between Colombia and Venezuela, I wouldn't be surprised if Colombia volunteered its regular army."

Peter had to agree with Denise's assessment; even the Venezuelan guards could be bought by Dane if he had the notion to do so.

"No, I don't want to add Dane to the contract. He's only the muscle. Andy is the brains." Peter was forever underestimating those who had served in the military. His belief was that if they had anything else going for them, they would have never volunteered for such an uninspiring career. "How long do you plan on staying in Caracas?"

"I plan on getting out as soon as possible. I don't know if Andy had a chance to put enough in motion to have a successful coup, but I can tell you this: the tension here will definitely lead to a riot or two, and I don't want to be that sad 'in the wrong place at the wrong time' statistic," Denise responded. "I'll be in touch when I land in a safe place."

Denise broke off the connection and went to check out of the hotel and get the hell out of Dodge.

Twenty-One

Denise wasn't far off the mark in her estimation of the tension that pervaded the Venezuelan air. In response to a popular elected representative being arrested for sedition, the citizens of Caracas filled the streets in the afternoon with protesters. People shouted and clashed with those who supported the government and Gomez. As the people poured into the streets, they were joined by a beautiful, popular actress. Christiana Vasquez was the darling of Venezuelans. Their love for her knew no bounds. Not only was she a talented actress, she had a generous heart. When she wasn't filming, she was donating her time and money to help those in the most impoverished parts of Venezuela. Even in the barrios, she walked unmolested. She was revered by those who lived there.

Christiana joined hands with those in the streets, demanding the release of their representative. The mass of humanity marched down the street, encouraging those who looked on to join them, vowing to take their fight directly to the president. Those who did not join the march gathered on the sidewalks to watch the protesters and shout encouragement. Police and federales stood watching the gathering but did not attempt to disband it.

In the end it was the most innocent thing that set off the riot. As the protesters passed through the narrow streets, they passed by a section where bars crowded one another, competing for patrons. At one of the bars, a drunk stumbled out. Slurring his words as he shouted out to the passing parade of activists, he tried to join the march but stumbled and dropped his glass of tequila. The glass shattered, spraying a nearby woman with shards of glass and alcohol.

She screamed at the top of her lungs, thinking that it had been thrown at her. Her screams reverberated among the marchers and the onlookers, and they heard the panic they communicated. In that flash of a moment—that snapshot of time—panic spread like an explosion through the crowd. Confusion and alarm quickly gripped those in the middle of the throng, who felt trapped by the narrow avenue.

Then they stampeded. Not clear about what was happening, those charged with keeping the protesters from going too far drew their weapons. One officer in particular drew a bead on the fearful Christiana Vasquez. He waited patiently, unmindful of the chaos around him, for the movement of the crowd to bring her closer. He counted the steps until she passed by him and then fired into her back. She fell.

Pandemonium ensued, and the officer melted into the mob. Protesters and onlookers fled down various streets until quiet descended on the street, and the only person left was a young man cradling the body of the once beautiful and vibrant actress.

Word quickly spread of Christiana's death, and Venezuela descended into mourning the loss of its favorite child. The stillness that embraced the country that late afternoon was thick with ominous tension. People whispered to one another in the barrios, on college campuses, and even in the more affluent sections of town. The hatred of this tyrannical government and its despotic ruler had reached a dangerous level. Now Venezuelans huddled in their homes as darkness fell, wondering if the revolutionaries would retaliate or if the death of Venezuela's favorite daughter would mobilize a full-fledged effort to overthrow the government.

Among those who were now scurrying through the streets to either join up with compatriots or find a safe place to keep their heads down, Dane moved with purpose. This city had turned into a powder keg, and he wasn't sure how much longer it would be before it blew completely, but he would be surprised if this pseudo peace lasted more than forty-eight hours.

The revolution was just gathering its strength, consolidating its power before it unleashed hell on earth. Dane felt this in his bones. He had been through enough of them to know. The window for people to leave the country was narrowing, though he doubted that many of the tourists frolicking in the ocean or taking in Angel Falls were even aware of the danger lurking beneath the surface.

Dane's job was not yet finished here, but Andy's was. It was time for him to leave before it became impossible. Dane was making his way to the other side of the city, toward the airport and the beachfront hotel where Andy was comfortably holed up. Dane had arranged for a boat to be located offshore from the hotel. Andy would leave by water, under the radar.

A big surprise to Dane came when the Venezuelan government issued an arrest warrant for Andy Wayne, US citizen and representative of the CLU, on charges that included murder and terrorism. The police broadcast went on to say that his whereabouts were unknown. Dane, however, knew where to find him; and very shortly, so would the Venezuelan government. When Dane first heard Andy's name being mentioned in the same sentence as an arrest warrant, he thought, *What the fuck?* There was no reason for the Venezuelan government to be looking at him. His short forays just over the border were limited to a select group of people who were, at the moment, still leading the bloody unrest. How did they get his name? Who pointed them to him?

Then it hit him. Denise, Peter Abercrombie's contract killer, must have alerted Venezuelan authorities. Now he was racing against the clock to get to Andy and get him out of the country. The repercussions that the United States would feel, as well as CLU, and by extension the American labor movement, would be huge.

The AFL-CIO had never publicly acknowledged its history with the CIA and the US government. Through outfits such as the CLU, a joint effort of American labor movements, the US government, and global corporations, the American trade unions had been involved for decades in shadowing the reactionary political aims of the US government. Instituted during the Cold War in 1961, under the protection of former AFL-CIO president George Meany, the Center for Labor Unity gave direct support to US-backed coups in Brazil, Argentina, and Chile. At that time, some people at the AFL-CIO were co-opted by the process. Others willingly joined, and still others remained oblivious to the extracurricular activities that the AFL-CIO indulged in.

After the botched attempt to overthrow Chavez in 2002, when the finger was pointed directly at the American labor movement, CLU had managed to keep itself out of the public eye, and that must be maintained at all costs. If the Venezuelans got to Andy before Dane could get him out of the country, then all hell would break loose in the media back home. The problem in some elected officials' eyes was that the CLU had rebuffed demands to be held answerable for its third-world actions and instead had favored functioning in the shadows globally—many times on behalf of US foreign-policy interests. If Venezuela took Andy into custody, the leap to believing the US was behind the coup would not be a big one to make.

Knowing all this, Dane focused immediately on getting Andy out.

The late afternoon was giving way to evening when Dane reached the Marriott Playa Grande. He had been glad to leave the city behind as the quiet that blanketed it was unnatural and it spooked him. He had commandeered a moped abandoned by the owner when the morning protests turned violent. Time was of the essence, and there wasn't a taxi to be found on the deadly quiet city streets.

He had never been so grateful to pull into the hotel's entrance as he was at that moment. The fact that his large, hulking physique looked ridiculous on the small Moped to those who watched his approach didn't faze him. You only found abandoned Harleys or BMWs in the movies.

The sun was setting in a glorious red and orange ball. Bright yellow streamers reached out from it, searing the turquoise sky in a spectacular light show. Dane was not observing it as he dumped the moped to the ground and half walked, half ran into the hotel. He hoped that Andy had seen the news and knew to keep a low profile. He normally locked himself in his room during the last couple of days as the heat built up inside a movement. Dane hoped he hadn't broken that habit.

It would be up to him to get Andy to the boat before anyone showed up looking for him. He waited impatiently outside of the elevator as it slowly descended to the lobby, stopping at several floors along the way. Dane cursed his luck. Why was it that when you were in a hurry, everything seemed to happen in slow motion? Using the stairs was a thought he quickly discarded as the number of floors he would have to go up would take more time than just waiting.

As soon as the doors opened, he jumped inside, rudely shoving the occupants as they scrambled to get out. He punched the floor number and then jabbed the close door button several times. He then decided that this had to be the slowest elevator ever created. The doors had barely opened when Dane shot out of it and ran toward Andy's room. He pulled up short when he saw the bullet holes through the door.

"Shit," he said under his breath.

He looked up and down the hall. There was no one around. He threw his shoulder into the door and heard the frame start to give way. Thank God it was a wood frame. It took him two more bone-jarring slams against the door before it gave way. He felt something move as he shoved the broken door inward. He looked down. Andy's crumpled form lay right in front of the door. He lay on his side, like his body had twisted as he fell after the bullets had hit him. There was a large stain where the carpet had soaked up the blood. Dane closed the broken door as much as he was able and bent over Andy's still form to see if he was still alive. Alive or dead, Dane would have to get him out of the hotel and into that boat. There could be no trace of CLU in this country.

There was a faint pulse. That was good, but he had lost a lot of blood. That was bad. Dane did the best he could, making a field dressing out of one of the top sheets. He turned Andy onto his back and propped him up a bit, using the hotel pillows. He picked up his phone and thought for a minute. He couldn't call Joyia. She had a very critical part of the plan to carry out and could not be pulled away from it. Marco, Francisco—everyone was scattered to the winds at this point. He was going to need some help getting Andy out of here, and the seventy-plus-year-old smuggler whose boat Dane had arranged to take them up the coast was not going to cut it.

He dialed Koshka's number.

Twenty-Two

D ane dialed Koshka's number into an encrypted sat phone and waited as it rang once before dumping him into her voice mail. Dane sat on the bed and waited—and watched. His mind played through different scenarios as to how he could get Andy out without any issues.

Dane pulled out his Colt M1911. It was the same handgun his father had carried in Vietnam. Colonel John T. Thompson of Army Ordnance put his signature on a letter to Colt's president proclaiming the Colt .45 automatic pistol as the official service handgun of the US Army on March 29, 1911.

In Dane's mind, his 1911 was his partner and closest friend. That good friend was now aimed in the direction of the hotel room door as it swung open and a dirty, exhausted, yet smiling Marco stumbled in.

At the sight of a gun pointed at him, Marco's smile suddenly faded, and his hands went up. His eyes went from the gun to Andy's prone figure on the floor and then up to Dane's face. Although Dane had never met Marco, Dane recognized him from the pictures that Andy had given him of their contacts in Venezuela.

"You're Marco," Dane stated.

Marco nodded enthusiastically, but he looked questioningly at Dane.

Understanding the look, Dane then said, "I'm Dane."

The look of relief that crossed Marco's face was followed by the question, "What happened to Andy?"

"I don't know. I just found him this way."

"I noticed the broken door." Marco pointed to the door behind him.

"I did that. I saw the bullet holes through the door and had to break in. I found him this way. I need some help getting him down to the dock. I've arranged for a boat to take us up the coast."

"Will he make it? He looks badly hurt," Marco observed.

"Alive or dead, it doesn't matter. He or his body can't be found in Venezuela."

Marco nodded in understanding. "I'll go get a wheelchair from the concierge desk. We can get him into that. Wrap him up in a blanket like an old man with a hat on. Do you have some sunglasses?"

"Yes. If we can get him down to the dock and get him in the boat, we'll be out of here."

Marco nodded. "I need to go get the chair now."

Dane looked down at Andy and saw some of the blood starting to seep through the bandage. He tore the fitted sheet off the bed and started tearing it into strips to add to what he had already wrapped around Andy's chest.

Dane fidgeted as he waited for what seemed like a pro-tracted length of time before Marco lightly knocked and then entered the room pushing a wheelchair.

"I have a doctor meeting us at the hotel dock," Marco said. "She is discreet and has helped us before when activists have gotten hurt by Gomez's thugs. The Catholic Church paid for her education, and she was working nearby in the barrio with those who had been injured in an earlier demonstration."

"She won't have time to do anything. We need to get on the boat."

"She'll go with you and make her way back. Please don't argue with me on this. He has done much to help us, and I won't let him die if I can help prevent it."

Dane grunted. "He knew the risks coming in." However, he didn't offer any further argument.

They carefully lifted Andy into the wheelchair. They posed him with his hands in his lap and a blanket wrapped around him. Dane settled Joyia's discarded floppy straw hat on Andy's head while Marco placed a pair of sunglasses over his eyes.

"Ready?" Dane asked.

Marco nodded, and they both set off, pushing the "old man" to the elevators.

They got to the end of the dock, and in the distance, Dane spotted a boat approaching at a moderate speed. He was pretty sure that was their ride, but it was still a little too far out to be certain. As they watched the boat approach, a female voice spoke from behind.

"Is this my patient?"

Dane turned toward the person asking the question. She had a weathered face and lively brown eyes. Dane placed her age to be around forty-five, maybe pushing fifty. Dane gave a curt nod. "You'll have to wait to examine him until we get on that boat." Dane pointed toward the boat that had gotten close enough for Dane to identify it.

"What happened?" she asked as she moved closer to Andy's still form.

"Shot twice in the chest. I hope he doesn't waste your time by dying on you."

If she was put off by Dane's clipped tone, she didn't show it.

When the small outboard pulled up to the dock, the old smuggler called out a greeting to the doctor in his native language, which she returned with a wide smile.

"You two know each other?" Dane asked as he positioned the wheelchair to make it easier to transfer Andy from the dock to the boat.

"The career path of a smuggler is a high-risk endeavor," she replied with a trace of humor in her voice.

Marco saluted the boat as it pulled away from the dock with its human cargo. Dane tipped his head in acknowledgment, but the doctor was already busy working on her patient.

Marco stood on the dock, watching the boat fade into an obscure dot on the horizon; then he turned to head back to the city. He wanted to make it back to his family compound as quickly as possible. It was already dark, and he could see the fires of rebellion burning hot all over the city. He was worried about his family's safety.

Twenty-Three

Venezuela suffered the world's fifth highest homicide rate, with forty-five out of every hundred thousand people killed in 2010, trailing only Honduras, El Salvador, the Ivory Coast, and Jamaica. That murder rate had doubled since 1999, when Chavez was first elected president. Kidnappings increased twenty-six-fold from 1999 to 2011.

The government refused to take action on any of these problems and would not admit to how bad things really were. Chavez's sycophants in the government bureaus stopped releasing official crime statistics in 2005, leaving it to nonprofit groups to sort through the wounded and dead.

When nonprofit representatives were asked to explain the motives behind the carnage, experts focused on one impression: impunity, and not just for street criminals, but also for police and politicians, who they said had intensified the crisis. Only 9 percent of homicides resulted in an arrest, and the police committed as much as a quarter of the country's crimes. And while the government did control countless neighborhood "collectives" that enforced political loyalty, those same groups often participated in street crime rather than protecting residents.

The frustration that roiled under the surface of this country of twenty-eight million people eclipsed the everyday fear—the fear that had been shaped by daily gun battles, kidnappings for ransom, and other criminal activity that permeated every breath the Venezuelan citizens collectively took. Whole neighborhoods were occupied with a new street life. Neighborhoods once abandoned at night now teemed with rebellion. While foreign diplomats wrung their hands with anxiety and worry concerning the possibility of offending a petty dictator, working-class Venezuelans, from farmers to students of the wealthiest families, were taking matters into their own hands.

Among all its miseries, including double-digit inflation, widespread crime, and disintegrating infrastructure, the decay of Venezuela was seen by many as the fault of the late President Hugo Chavez's government—and one that a whole generation of this shell-shocked country had decided to correct on this night.

The protests started almost without anyone noticing. In the darkened streets of the ghettos, the black-clad multitudes, their faces covered with masks, moved like one massive organism down the expanse of dank, narrow alleys past the zinc roofs of shanties, some built four stories tall. The scene was being played out simultaneously in Caracas, Puerto Cabello, Valencia, Chacao, Maracay, and many other cities in Venezuela.

Smaller towns set up barricades on the roads, while those in the more populated areas set up blockades at street intersections. Stray bullets flew through the air and hooligans on motorcycles sped through the streets; and people within Venezuela peeked out at the marauding mob from their windows as nightfall blanketed the country in darkness.

From above, unseen and unnoticed, a satellite's camera lens gazed down at the sea of slum roofs as it recorded the rise of a revolution. Tonight the Venezuelans were once again at war with one another.

Public security policy in Venezuela had traditionally been very weak. Andy knew this, as did the leaders of the mass of angry humanity that was surging through the streets of Venezuela. Caracas was a prominent example of the broken chain of command that existed within the government and its enforcement apparatus. The city used to run its own police force, in conjunction with those of its five independent municipalities. After Caracas's mayor began clashing with the late president, Chavez replaced citywide police with a national force but brought in only twelve thousand officers, most of them based in Caracas. By contrast, the phased-out force had been nearly double that number.

Instead of solving the problem, Chavez would only say that criminality was a result of poverty, which was a consequence of capitalism. So while Gomez had Chavez to thank for the power he now held, he also had Chavez to thank for his imminent humiliating overthrow. Those phased-out police officers were now mingling with the crowd, some as honest protesters and members of the opposition, others as hired agitators.

When handed the reins of power, Gomez could have made an effort to repair the state of law enforcement, but like his predecessor, he blamed it on capitalism while also claiming that the poverty level had dropped.

But that excuse no longer rested easy on the ears of the once faithful. The oil-rich country had been tormented by an inflation rate of nearly 60 percent. Venezuelans had agonized over shortages of basic foods, goods, and medicine for over a decade now, but upon Gomez's questionable election win, the country's population saw new levels of scarcity. The Venezuelan government now admitted that one in four basic goods was out of stock. The truth, however, was much worse.

The sea of people roared with approval at the words that a man had shouted out over a megaphone. The anger had been building for years among the citizenry.

The floodlights of the palace cut through the darkness as the protesters started throwing rocks and bottles at the fences. Screams echoed from the crowds as a surge of humanity pushed against the gates.

Suddenly a shot rang out, and a young man fell. A woman covered his body with a coat.

Amid the confusion and the hate, Venezuela erupted. Across the country, towns and cities convulsed in a cataclysm of violence as the government of President Gomez tried to enforce a brutal crackdown. Streets echoed to the explosions of gunfire, water cannons, and tear-gas canisters as national guard units and national police came out in force.

Most frightening were the gangs of paramilitary fighters who flooded neighborhoods on motorcycles and appeared to act with impunity. Mobs of regime supporters—paramilitary gangs known as *colectivos*—circled neighborhoods and public squares on their motorcycles, firing their guns at anyone who lingered in the open. Some stampeded into apartment buildings to hunt for opposition protesters. There were even reports trickling out about torture.

The crackdown extended from Caracas to Maracaibo, Maracay, Valencia, and nearly every major city across the country. Venezuela's cities had become notoriously dangerous in recent years, as the country's crime and murder rate soared, but on this night, Venezuelan cities weren't simply dangerous—they were war zones.

Gomez had never possessed his predecessor's poise, communication skills, or political shrewdness, and he inherited a government rampant with corruption. Since his narrow election, the fear had been that Chavismo's strange balance of bluster and self-doubt would fluctuate madly in his hands, especially as the country's ominous economic circumstances deteriorated.

The government reacted to the wave of opposition protests that broke out across the country with a heavy-handedness that even Chavez had refrained from using. Tonight's government crackdown was the most violent since the protests and riots that had overwhelmed the country in 1989. Chacao, a wealth district of Caracas, saw fanatical fighting, with protesters lobbing rocks and Molotov cocktails at national guard units, who responded with tear-gas canisters and buckshot.

San Cristobal experienced some of the worst clashes, and President Gomez even threatened to have the mayor, also a member of the opposition, tossed into prison. Chavistas had long raised the specter of civil war if political contests didn't go their way, but tonight they got a taste of their own medicine.

The situation in the country deteriorated so quickly and was so bloody that airlines refused to fly there. The flight boards across the world's airports lit up with cancellations. Venezuela was wounded and bleeding.

The demonstrations energized the opposition, and they put the presidential palace under siege. The violence continued to batter the country through the weekend with raucous demonstrations around Caracas and various provincial cities. On Wednesday, the protests once again turned deadly, and twenty-three people were fatally shot. One was a six-year-old girl on her way home from her grandmother's. The child's mother was critically injured. Fingers were pointed at the Venezuelan military for having fired the fatal shot, and the army now found itself overwhelmed by crazed mobs.

The protests shook the core of Venezuela. But protest was too mild a word. The viciousness of the demonstrations struck deep into the belly of the Venezuelan government. And much to the concern of Gomez, the ferocity of the attacks was gaining in strength, not weakening. Underneath the chaos, he believed he saw the structure of a well-thought-out coup. Wasn't this what it looked like when Chavez originally rose to power? The question ricocheted around in his head as panic swelled within him.

Venezuelan students and those who marched out from under the blanket of poverty that covered the barrios swore to stay in the streets until Gomez resigned, though the fifty-five-year-old former military man and revolutionary has declared that he would not cede even a "smidgen" of power.

In the past, protests in Caracas had typically been restricted to fashionable areas, but this time Venezuelans from all walks joined them en masse. From the balcony of Miraflores, it was easy for Gomez to believe that the entire nation of twenty-eight million people was waging war on its government.

In Maracaibo, a city larger than Caracas, the poor had amassed and blocked several avenues into the affluent neighborhoods of government officials.

In the small town of San Mateo, farmers dumped the offal from their livestock in the city square and lit it on fire. Dissenting students in the Andean city of San Cristobal burned tires, while citizens reported massive riots in Merida and on the island of Margarita.

Venezuelan Socialist Party workers said armed military intelligence officers burst into their premises, seeking the national coordinator. They found him hiding beneath a desk and promptly shot him. Videos sent to the media by an anonymous bystander showed men in military garb entering the building, gesticulating wildly with their guns and trying to kick down a door to an inner office. Why the military would turn on the Socialist Party seemed to be a mystery. But it was held up as proof that Gomez and his military thugs were out of control and were now massacring even their allies in a bloody free-for-all.

The mayor of San Cristobal was arrested as well as the mayor of Caracas. Several elected political officials found themselves looking down the barrels of rifles and pistols as they were arrested and marched off to prison for the crime of treason and supporting the overthrow of the Gomez government.

The Venezuelan government was pointing the finger at the United States as it continued to issue press releases to excuse the brutality it was inflicting on its own people.

Twenty-Four

By sunrise the next day, the violence had abated, allowing for protesters carrying signs for democracy to occupy the streets where blood had been let the night before. They demanded justice for those who had been slaughtered by the Venezuelan police and the release of all political prisoners.

The marches lasted through the afternoon. In the street where Christiana Vasquez had been shot in the back, a memorial of flowers and handmade cards stood as a reminder of a country's fallen innocence. Wails of those who mourned the loss of family and loved ones echoed through the allies of the barrios and through the streets of a city whose pockmarked buildings stood as witnesses to the violence done the night before.

Every bit of news sucked up by the reporters and cameramen got fed into the twenty-four-hour media machine for the world to ingest in overwhelming quantities. The AP reported as follows:

At midnight, a new Venezuelan student movement emerged that has grabbed headlines domestically and internationally. Thousands took to the streets, some marching peacefully and some squaring off against the police with rocks and bullets, all in the name of "freedom of expression." During the night Venezuela was rocked by violent protests that left many dead in the street, including Venezuela's most beloved actress, Christiana Vasquez. Venezuelan President Miguel Gomez spoke to the press, stating, "We want to denounce today a campaign that intends to convince the country that these student protests are spontaneous, civil, peaceful, and democratic. But behind them there lies an entire conspiratorial apparatus. The elitist rich and their American partners are using these kids as cannon fodder..."

His words rang hollow to the press, to the world, and to his own people. As the day quickly passed and night reclaimed the country once again, those who mourned their losses were once again replaced by those who sought vengeance for those same losses—only this time, those seeking revenge had grown in number. Once again violence ruled the streets, and once again the journalists sent back their stories and film of the unfolding coup to their news agencies. Their stories reeked of condemnation for the Gomez government's viciousness and its violation of human rights. As the night played out, Gomez's henchman responded to the media's negative coverage by arresting and beating nine journalists. Cameras and other equipment were confiscated or destroyed. Three of the journalists were from Britain, France, and Canada. American photojournalist Lindsey Rutgers was hit in the head with a pistol, shot with rubber bullets, and had a rib broken by Venezuelan police.

German freelance photojournalist Fritz Krieger was snapping photos of the violence and the wholesale slaughter of people demonstrating in the main thoroughfare when a soldier in the Venezuelan army snatched his camera from his hands. Fritz had been through the world's war zones before, and this was not the first time his camera had been snatched. That was why he uploaded to his cloud as he shot photos and why he was always changing out his memory card so that when this happened, he would still have some photos and not be left empty-handed.

However, Krieger could not refrain from launching several cuss words in Spanish at the soldier. The soldier responded, but there was something off about his speech. The words were not quite right. Fritz should have known to keep his mouth shut, but in the heat of the moment, he screamed at the soldier, "You're not Venezuelan. What are you? Colombian, Brazilian?"

Those would be Fritz's last words. The soldier swung the barrel of his AK-47 around and fired into Fritz Krieger's chest and head. There was not much left of the photojournalist, and he would later be identified only by the credentials in his wallet. He would be listed as just another casualty in the war for freedom in South America—another journalist dying while attempting to record history as it unfolded.

The world watched as Venezuela burned; then it reacted. Venezuela's highly traded global bonds, which fluctuated sharply on civil unrest or political tension, plummeted to an all-time low as those who held them looked for buyers to dump them on. And those who truly understood the orchestrated events bought the bonds up at bargain basement prices, knowing that in the end, the bonds would rebound to all-time highs. But only those rich enough or politically connected enough understood what was truly happening in Venezuela.

After seven days of unfettered bloodletting by the military and the rampaging civilian population, activists from the World Health Organization and the United Nations began to say that some detained demonstrators had been tortured, while videos and photos circulating online showed uniformed men firing on protesters. Gomez insisted the military had been restrained in the face of incitement and assaults, but with the videos and pictures going viral, his protests of innocence were drowned out by demands that he step down. Cuba offered asylum. Gomez refused.

Leaders from around the world denounced the government violence while the government accused the rioters of vandalizing buildings and burning trash in the city streets. Hooded protesters wearing Guy Fawkes masks and dressed in identical black clothing gathered outside the headquarters of state TV channel VT, lighting fires in the streets and hurling stones and Molotov cocktails. Their masks took on an eerie glow as they reflected the light from the flames of burning buildings.

On the tenth night of riots and bloodshed, as crowds amassed and started heading for the presidential palace, Joyia Gabriella looked singularly attractive in her Venezuelan National Police uniform as she skidded the Jeep to a halt inside the inner courtyard of Miraflores.

She jumped out of the Jeep, screaming, "*El presidente, el presidente!*"

As she ran up the stairs to the palace, the Venezuelan guards who, up to this point, had been nervously stationed on the steps followed her into the palace. Neither of them bothered to ask her for any credentials. In the panic, neither young recruit ever even thought that anyone could be masquerading as the police. Their government demanded absolute obedience from its citizens, so most soldiers could not conceive of a citizen being brave enough to falsely pass him- or herself off as an official, especially a woman. To be caught doing such a thing would be punishable by death.

President Gomez heard the strident cries of a female calling his name and rushed into the central hallway.

Joyia stopped and saluted smartly, pushing her breasts out as she did so. The movement and its results were not lost on the males surrounding her.

"President Gomez," Joyia said breathlessly. "The filthy opposition rioters move toward the palace. It is time to move you to a safe place."

"I will not surrender to this human garbage. I am president!" Gomez responded. "I am president. I will kill them all!"

His declaration was met by an exploding Molotov cocktail in the inner courtyard. The mob had reached the gates and was intent on bringing them down. The gates were all that separated them from the president they loathed.

President Gomez's bravado wilted quickly in the face of what he was sure would be his death.

Joyia read the expressions on the man's face and quickly seized the moment. "Come now."

She ushered the president into a waiting jeep. When the soldiers guarding the palace attempted to get into the jeep, Joyia quickly castigated them for their actions. "You must remain and fight for Chavismo. Are our soldiers frightened women or armed men? Shoot them, you idiots, while I get our president to safety."

With that, she spun the wheel on the jeep while hitting the gas and sped off through the back gates.

The soldiers turned to face the angry mob pushing on the gates; then they broke and ran into the palace. Neither the guards nor the president realized that behind the mob of angry people, the military was now moving in. From the rear of the angry mass, the Venezuelan soldiers started firing, and bodies began to fall. By the time the military broke through and the people left alive had scattered, President Gomez and the attractive female police officer were long gone, and no one could say where they went or even provide a name for the woman he had gone with.

Joyia headed out of Caracas with a terrified President Gomez seated next to her. His white-knuckled grip on the military jeep's windshield revealed just how terrified the man was.

"Where are we headed?" he asked his attractive driver.

"I am taking you to safety," she responded. "We have a stronghold established just outside of Maracaibo. You will be safe there until we put down the rebellion."

Joyia arrived with President Gomez in Maracaibo around midnight. Taking the back roads into the city, she came to a halt in front of a darkened farmhouse. Outside of the farmhouse, Gomez could see the shadowed images of Venezuelan soldiers and felt better about his impetuous flight from the presidential palace. He got out of the jeep, and the soldier nearest the door turned to him and saluted smartly. President Gomez returned the salute with a curt nod as he ducked his head to avoid bumping it on the low entryway. Inside the house, a man waited until Gomez's head was completely inside the doorway before he slammed it with a large sledgehammer.

The man walked outside the farmhouse and up to Joyia.

"It is done," he said as he lit a cigarette.

She smiled. "Help me stuff him into this trunk, and I'll get him into Colombia before I dump his body." She pointed to a large steamer trunk in the back of the jeep.

"No, senorita, tonight you rest. The border will be crawling with real Venezuelan soldiers looking for people like you going back and forth across the border under the cover of darkness. We have a better way to get you across."

She acquiesced to the revolutionary's suggestion and spent the night on a straw mattress in the farmhouse.

The Colombian border was some three hours away from the farmhouse outside of Maracaibo, and the rebels had arranged for a shared "colectivo" from the bus station to take Joyia with her trunk stuffed with the body of the Venezuelan president to the border.

These colectivos were revamped cars from the United States. Most were cars that had been totaled out by US insurers and sold to companies who specialized in exporting the cars to third-world countries. The import and export fees were ridiculously low on these vehicles. Once they made it to a South American country, they were refitted with any manner of materials needed to get them running.

The car they got to transport Joyia and her cargo was in the worst condition Joyia had seen yet. It had no passenger windows, just the front and rear windows, and Joyia could see straight through the bare metalwork of her door to the passing road below. Normally these "taxis" would be shared by several people in order to defray the cost, but in this case, three of the phony Venezuelan soldiers would share the ride with her to give her some protection to the border.

The colectivo was driven by a mean-looking guy who reminded Joyia of a retired boxer with a chip on his shoulder. The four men accompanying Joyia became quite defensive when it appeared the military police wanted to check her trunk. Tensions were defused when Joyia offered the police officers a handsome bribe to let them pass.

Other than the dubious interests of the military police, Joyia's journey was uneventful, and the driver negotiated the border crossings through Zulia with ease and crossed over into Colombia.

With the main population centers of Venezuela being swallowed by civil unrest and violence, the Venezuelan army found better places to stage their troops than stopping those who wished to leave their country. Even before the outbreak of violence in Venezuela, the border between Venezuela and

Colombia was limited to locals and drug cartels. The US State Department website advised against all travel to within fifty miles of the Colombian border in the states of Zulia, Tǎchira, and Apure. Drug traffickers and illegal armed groups were active in these states, and there was a risk of kidnapping. It was this very element that assured Joyia's success in getting the Venezuelan president's body into Colombia without any additional interference.

After two weeks of violent demonstrations and riots, the UN declared that Venezuela had disintegrated into a full-fledged civil war. The whereabouts of President Gomez was unknown.

With the disappearance of Gomez, the overthrow of the government was all but complete. The brutality and the bloodshed would make their way into the forgotten annals of history as the corporate world circled like vultures, waiting for the last breath from the shredded beast of what was left of the Chavismo government. Soon they would swoop in to help the new capitalist government not only get established but also be successful. They would keep them propped up as the new leaders cemented their power over the oil-rich nation. Oil companies would have their property returned to them, and government-owned entities would be privatized. Of course, their new owners would be those who had not only been on the right side of the political upheaval but also had the money they needed to curry favor with the newly installed leadership.

Twenty-Five

The Venezuelan smuggler had dropped off his human cargo in the coastal city of Santa Marta, Colombia. Santa Marta was the oldest city in Colombia as well as the third largest. Fringed by beautiful beaches and the stunning mountains of the Sierra Nevada de Santa Marta range, it was a romantic destination for lovers from all over the world.

Dane was not here for romance, however, so his appreciation of the lush mangroves and the picturesque tropical setting was subdued, to say the least. During the boat ride, Andy had weaved in and out of consciousness. When he was conscious, he was only slightly lucid.

They were met on the beach by one of Dane's contacts from the past, a retired mercenary who took the money he had saved and bought a banana plantation just outside of the city. After that, he promptly married a young senorita half his age from a well-connected family and started filling the plantation with his own progeny.

He provided Dane and his group a place to stay in a little casita on the plantation, secluded from the main house. Once they were safely settled into their lodgings, Dane took more of an interest in the doctor, who was making every effort to stabilize Andy's condition.

"Do you have a name, or do I just call you Doc?" Dane asked.

The woman smiled that same steady, serene smile. "You can call me Doctor Mary Katherine, or you can call me Sister Mary Katherine. I answer to both," she replied.

Dane's brows rose in surprise. He had never thought about a nun becoming a doctor—or was it vice versa? Before he got the chance to ask, his phone rang. He looked down and saw that it was Koshka, so he excused himself and walked outside the casita to take the call privately.

"How bad is he?" Koshka asked as soon as Dane hit the answer button. Obviously, she had taken the time to listen to his voice mail prior to calling him back.

"The doctor is trying to stabilize him now," Dane replied. He then gave Koshka a complete rundown on finding Andy in the hotel room, Marco's appearance and assistance in moving Andy to the boat, and his call to a trusted doctor to try to keep Andy alive until they could get him to a medical facility.

Koshka listened without interrupting. "Where are you now?"

"We're holed up at Tony's."

Koshka knew of the banana plantation and its owner. They had crossed paths years ago in another time and place. "Does he have an airstrip?"

"Yes. He's got a strip big enough for a small Cessna, but you're going to have to send a doctor, or we have to take the one we got, because he took a couple bullets to the chest. He lost a lot of blood. Good thing the doctor here is experienced in what she calls barrio triage. She has dealt with this type of injury before many times, but I'll feel better once we're on our own soil."

"Understood. Try to keep him alive. I'll be sending a plane and a doctor. It should land tomorrow late morning, early afternoon."

Dane nodded. "Will do."

"Dane?"

"Yeah?"

"Make sure the doctor leaves well compensated, and I want her contact information. We take care of those who take care of us."

"She's a nun," Dane said without knowing why he said it.

The silence on the other end of the line made him realize that Koshka, too, was wondering why he had just made that statement.

"I'll get the info," he finished somewhat lamely and ended the call.

When he entered the casita, the doctor nun, as he had started to think of her, had stripped off Andy's clothes to the waist, leaving him bare-chested. She had her medical bag open and several surgical instruments placed on the bedside table. One of those instruments was a scalpel.

"What are you doing?" he asked as he walked over.

She responded without looking up. "Come here and look at this."

Dane walked over and looked at Andy's chest. There were two bullet holes, and he could see where she had cleaned them up, removing the dried blood. He looked at the hole that was squarely over Andy's heart, where the doctor nun was pointing with the scalpel she held in her hand. At first he couldn't tell what she was looking at with such interest, but then he saw it. Once the wound was cleaned, you could see a part of the bullet that had entered the chest.

He turned and looked at the diminutive woman standing next to him. "It didn't go in very far."

"No, indeed it did not. I couldn't tell you why, but something stopped its momentum."

"He was shot through a door. Is the other bullet as close to the surface?"

"No. I'm afraid not. That one is much deeper, but for whatever reason, the kill shot ended up failing to penetrate past the outer muscle."

He thought it was weird to hear a nun use the term "kill shot." He wondered how long she had been patching up the shadier elements of the Caracas barrios and why she would pursue that work in the first place.

"I'm going to extract the shallow bullet and flush out the wound. I don't think it'll need stitches, but we'll bandage it up good and tight. As for the other one, I can attempt to extract it, but if you're planning to move him quickly to a medical facility, it may be better to wait anyway. It would be a safer procedure with modern technology, such as an X-ray machine, than me digging in there that close to his heart."

Dane nodded. "Do you need me to do anything?"

"You can get me some clean water," she responded.

He set the water down on the table and watched her finish placing a protective covering over the bullet she was leaving in Andy's chest. She thanked him as she turned her attention toward the other bullet. The skin had puckered, and the blood surrounding the bullet had dried, creating an adhesion between the bullet and the skin. She took a filled syringe from the table next to her and gave Andy a shot of morphine.

She waited a moment to give the sedative time to work its way through his system; then, using her scalpel and forceps, Dr. Mary Katherine worked at breaking the seal and pulling the projectile out. As she wiggled the object back and forth, Andy's eyes opened slightly, and he groaned in pain, showing that the morphine had not had enough time to take full effect, but it did dull the pain.

"I know it hurts, my dear, but it'll soon be over," she reassured him.

As she pulled, the bullet made a small sucking sound as the skin finally relinquished its grip on it. It also provoked a cry of pain from Andy as he tried to sit up. Dr. Mary Katherine laid a gentle hand and pushed him back down. She made soft reassuring noises to him. If she spoke any words, they were too soft for Dane to make out. Andy finally succumbed to the powerful pull of the morphine and was out.

Dane studied her as she cleansed the wound and poured some whiskey over it. She was slight of build and so tiny. Dane was sure that she didn't even reach five foot three. Feeling the need for some reason to break the silence, he asked her, "What made you become a nun and a doctor?"

"I came from a good family. Upper-class, Catholic. It was expected that I would marry my father's business partner's son. My life had been planned out, and I was content with that. My father and his partner, they were rebels at heart," she said with a wistful smile on her face. "When Chavez came to power, they fought him at every turn. Eventually Chavez had enough, and he seized my father's business and all our family's assets. His partner suffered the same fate. We moved into the barrios, and they accepted us there, but my father—for a while he was a broken man. Then my mother, the love of his life, his heart, she became ill. Socialism does not take care of the poor. It only entrenches the political class more deeply in control of the people. There were no doctors of worth who would treat her. The government health care, they decided that she did not have many productive years left, that the cost of her medical treatment outweighed what she could contribute to society, so she was denied care. She died.

"My father found his fight again, and they were a part of the 2002 coup to remove Chavez. He died, as did his partner and my intended. So I became a nun first to minister to the barrio, to give hope when there is none to be found, to inspire the populace with tales from the Bible of David and Goliath, and Daniel in the den of lions. I became a doctor to heal their wounds so they could fight another day, to give them comfort when they are sick so that they can become healthy."

"Has God given you the solace you sought?" Dane asked.

Dr. Mary Katherine gave a small laugh. "You are mistaken, my friend. I didn't do this to find peace. I did this to seek revenge. Through God I find the spiritual strength to fight and to inspire that same spirit of fight in others, and through medicine I find the knowledge to heal their bodies so they can carry out what their fighting spirits wish to accomplish."

Dane looked at her in surprise.

"Are you surprised at my words?" she said. "Don't be. 'Vengeance is mine, sayeth the Lord,' and his vengeance is a terrible thing to behold. However, with the world as it is, he is busy, so he sent me."

Dane chuckled, and she smiled back at him.

"There is more mettle to you then it would first appear," said Dane. "Is he going to be OK?"

"Well, he hasn't given up the ghost yet. He's a fighter. He has a low-grade fever, and I'll give him some antibiotics to hold him over. He'll need a real hospital, though, as quickly as it can be arranged. When he next awakens, we should try to get some liquids in him."

"Mary Kat," Dane said. "I need to know how to contact you. My boss wants to make sure that you are taken care of."

"I appreciate the consideration. Since the Good Lord frowns on pride, I do not have so much pride that I will turn down money. After all, spirituality feeds the soul, but it takes money for the more physical aspects."

Dane decided that he liked the doctor nun very much. She wrote her information on a piece of paper, and Dane put it into his wallet.

By morning Andy had awakened, and although he was weak from his ordeal and the low-grade fever, he was speaking. This, Dane thought, was an unfortunate turn of events as the only thing Andy was saying was that he would never forgive anyone for allowing him to be shot. Doctor Mary Katherine cautioned them both that Andy was not out of the woods yet. He still had a bullet in him; he had lost a lot of blood, and the risk of infection was high, especially as he was so weak.

The nun continued to pour liquids into him and provided a makeshift bedpan as she wanted him to move as little as possible. Both actions only elicited more complaints from Andy. However, he admitted to himself that he wasn't feeling so hot, and the idea of moving seemed to require more energy than he had.

By late morning, Andy's fever had hit full force, and Mary Katherine was sure that there was an infection that had developed. She gave him some pain pills to knock him out and kept wiping him down with cloth dipped in cold water to try to keep his body temperature from reaching a crisis stage.

In the early afternoon, a Cessna Citation M2 with two powerful Williams FJ44 engines touched down on the plantation's private runway. There were no markings on its sleek white fuselage. Dane figured that it was CIA. The small jet came complete with a doctor, and as soon as Andy was loaded, he was attaching tubes and other medical apparatus to him. The doctor talked with Mary Katherine to get an idea of how Andy's condition had progressed, and she clued him in and gave him a rundown of what she had done.

Dane made arrangements with Tony to get the good doctor nun back to her native soil.

"Mary Kat," he said, giving her a salute, "I will be seeing you again. Count on it."

She returned his salute. "You know where to find me now," she answered and then held up the envelope clutched in her hand. "Thank you for the donation to my clinic."

"That is just a token. It's all I had on me. We will be showing our full appreciation, so keep an eye out."

Dane nodded as he turned and trotted up the steps to the jet. Doctor Mary Katherine watched the jet taxi down the runway and then watched as it lifted off into the sky, disappearing behind an errant cloud.

Twenty-Six

Koshka leaned back in her chair as she scanned the interior of the Hawk and Dove. The few scattered patrons saved it from being empty, as the lunch hour was over, and most of those who worked at the Supreme Court or Library of Congress had already returned to work. There were few restaurants in the area, but Koshka still wondered, why even pick one in downtown DC? There was Georgetown, with its many cafés and bistros that appealed to Koshka more, but it had not been her choice—she wasn't even asked.

The day was blustery, and the place had a working fireplace with flames dancing in it to ward off the chill. The ambiance was good.

The Hawk and Dove was one of the oldest eateries and possibly the most famous. Its doors on Pennsylvania Avenue had opened to congressman, senators, journalists, and lobbyists. Deals and secrets were made and shared within its historical walls.

Lost in her study of the place, Koshka did not notice the man's arrival.

"I was a fan of the old Hawk, with its rabbit warren of small rooms scattered throughout the two floors." The man stopped and appeared to sniff the air. "I miss the damp and musty smell, pitchers of beer priced for an intern's budget, nooks where you could hide who you were meeting with."

Ezekiel lowered himself into the chair opposite Koshka with a grace that barely concealed a predator's movement. It was the first time that Koshka noticed the muscles in his biceps as they pushed against his suit jacket. She never took him to be a physical man, but maybe she had misread him.

A young server made her way to the table quickly to take the drink order.

"I think I'll have a Chocolate City." Ezekiel then turned to Koshka. "You should try one, or have a Flying Dog. Both are rather good local brews."

Koshka held up her glass. "I am already enjoying a Prosecco, but thank you for the recommendation."

"Prosecco is another of my favorites," Ezekiel acknowledged as he turned from the retreating wait staff to address Koshka. "But only when I am celebrating."

"But I am celebrating," Koshka replied. "Or haven't you heard? The Venezuelan government has been toppled."

Ezekiel quickly gave Koshka an assessment. The icy blue-eyed blonde met his gaze with a cocky look but did not seem overly put out by Ezekiel's study of her.

Ezekiel was prevented from responding as the waitress came to the table, set down his drink, and asked if they were ready to order.

They both ordered, and then the discussion resumed once the waitress had left.

"Did you not lose a man? Hardly a reason to celebrate. Unless, of course, you were planning on firing him; then it was quite a convenient turn of events."

"We all know the risks that come with the job. CLU has lost agents. We lost one in Nicaragua not too long ago when he was organizing the workers. Besides, I didn't lose him. He was merely shot."

"I am sure he would not view it as such."

"Well, Andy always was a bit of a prima donna."

Ezekiel smiled with his lips pursed together.

"Just why did you want to meet, Ezekiel?" Koshka asked, coming close to losing her patience with the verbal parrying.

"I was curious as to where we were with Cuba, and to be honest, I had so much on my plate with the various senators and congressman, I thought to multitask and have you meet me here. It saves me a trip to you, and I can eat at the same time."

"Ezekiel, I don't believe you. You are an evil, wicked man."

He issued a throaty chuckle. "And what are you, Koshka? You believe that some people are truly better than others. You view those who are poor or on welfare as a subhuman life form. You think communism is a fantastic form of government—with some tweaking, of course. Yet you just engineered the overthrow of a socialist government. What about it, Koshka? Is socialism not pure enough in its philosophy for you?"

She smiled, but it did not reach her eyes. "Socialism is just a gentler form of communism. I have nothing against it.

Only against governments who rebuke the authority of the Board and the US's leadership role on that Board. They cannot be allowed to stand. As far as socialism and the welfare state, yes, I do have issues with those who choose not to take care of themselves. I don't mind helping the helpless, just the clueless. It shows a lack of self-reliance, which I see as a flaw in their breeding. What other form of life would willingly allow themselves to be—for a lack of a better word—enslaved by others because they covet what others have instead of working for it themselves? People will get the politicians they elect, and a country will get the government it deserves. However, since they are inferior, I do have enough compassion to feed and shelter them, much as one would do with a stray dog or cat."

Ezekiel's sherry-colored eyes studied her for a moment.

"How is Andrew?" he finally asked.

"They say he will survive. I hope to have him back on his feet soon. However, that does bring up another issue."

"And what issue is that?"

"Peter Abercrombie and Denise Merron," Koshka responded. "They are responsible for trying to sabotage the Board's orders."

Ezekiel nodded as he stared into his beer. "Yes, it appears that they have crossed a line."

"Is that all you have to say?" Koshka demanded.

Again the conversation stopped as the waitress delivered the food to their table. She smiled at them both and asked in a cheerful voice, "Is there anything else I can get you?"

They both declined, and she walked away to serve another table.

"I will take care of it, Koshka. You need to concentrate on Cuba. Andy's absence will be sorely missed, and in his absence, another must stand in. Failure is never an option." At this point Ezekiel paused and gave Koshka a hard stare. "Take care how you address me, Koshka. I can still destroy you with just a word."

Koshka stopped chewing her food and looked at him for a long moment. "Are you threatening me, Ezekiel?"

"Why, yes; yes, I am. You consider Dane, Andy, Agnes, and the lot your people, and I doubt you would tolerate such insolence from them. However, you are my people, and I can raise you up or crush you beneath my boot. Never forget that, will you, my dear?" His voice sounded so polite, but the message was anything but.

Koshka was speechless in that moment as she watched him nonchalantly take a bite of his sandwich.

"And if I challenge you?"

"I did not take you for a fool," he responded. Then his face softened somewhat. "You must trust that I will take care of the matter."

She said nothing to that.

"I was reading an interesting paper put together by a professor from George Washington University," Ezekiel stated, as if the recent exchange never happened. "He believes that the United States will eventually be Balkanized. I thought that a rather profound statement to make."

"Indeed," Koshka responded, not quite over the threat Ezekiel had just made.

"Yes. He stated that he felt that the polarization of the American people was too far along to ever correct; however, he did not think it would lead to a war. No. He feels that we will fall apart, much like the old USSR."

The silence was deafening as Koshka refused to indulge Ezekiel in conversation. Finally she paused from eating her lunch and asked, "You don't care for me very much, do you, Ezekiel?"

"On the contrary, you hold the position you hold because of my recommendation," Ezekiel stated between bites of his lunch.

He offered a smile at her look of surprise and disbelief.

"Koshka, I spend my days working with politicians and other world leaders as well as the titans of the corporate class. I find you refreshingly direct in a realm of duplicity, and I say that as a compliment. You ask for no quarter, and you give none. Others find you complex because they are trying to see what your real motive is—what your angle is. What they fail to realize—and what I soon found out—was that with you, what you see is what you get. I enjoy the reprieve from the backstabbing and the mind games. While I may not agree with your opinions or even like you as a person, your straightforwardness is refreshing."

"Why is Cuba so important?" she asked. "I would think that the Middle East would warrant more attention."

Ezekiel used a napkin to wipe his lips and leaned back in the booth. "I would think that is obvious. We already have had one imbecilic president talk about giving Guantanamo back to Cuba; the risk is now elevated because that chip has been tossed onto the poker table. If Cuba, with its present government, reclaims Guantanamo, then what would stop it from giving it to Russia to use as a military base? Russians with ballistic missiles sixty miles off the Florida coast? While the thought holds a certain charm for an adrenalin junkie, it certainly would make this country's security agencies apoplectic. And needless to say what it would do to the tourism industry in the Keys. I can't even imagine how a PR firm would market that."

Koshka thought about his words for a minute. "There is a healthy core of resistance within Cuba, but they are very disorganized and have not had the benefits of a center to teach them anything. It would take much longer than Venezuela. We never left Venezuela."

"Understood. Perhaps this would be a good place for Joyia to improve her résumé," Ezekiel offered.

Koshka nodded. "Yes, as soon as we find her."

"Good. You take care of what you are good at and leave me to take care of the areas I excel in." Ezekiel offered Koshka the first genuine smile she had ever seen on the man's face.

Koshka walked briskly down Pennsylvania Avenue. Her hands were clad in soft lambskin gloves, and her body was shielded from the chilly air by her soft suede jacket. She was smiling. Anyone who passed her would mistakenly think that smile was an expression of happiness shown by a stunning-looking older woman, but it was in fact a smile of satisfaction. With the situation of Peter Abercrombie and Denise Merron in capable hands, Koshka could at least put the beginning of that operation on the back burner and concentrate on the truly critical issues: Cuba, Andy Wayne, and transitioning Venezuela to the capable hands of the CIA and the State Department.

Twenty-Seven

Six Months Later

In Seattle, Pioneer Square to be exact, there is something called the Underground Tour. This tour takes inquisitive tourists, amateur historians, and other students of Seattle's history through a labyrinth of tunnels that connect the buildings of old Seattle, which the new Seattle is built on. Most people are unaware of its existence or the fact that Seattle once sat at a lower elevation when it was originally built.

Seattle's first buildings, like many of the time, were wooden. However, like the great fire that scorched Chicago, Seattle, too, had the misfortune of a fire. A cabinetmaker accidently ignited a glue pot and then made a valiant attempt to extinguish it with water. Sadly, that method only spread the fire. So on June 6, 1889, at 2:39 p.m., what started as a small matter turned into a catastrophe as the fire was fed by the wooden buildings surrounding the cabinetmaker's shop. With the fire chief out of town, the volunteer fire department responded and made the mistake of trying to use too many hoses at once. They never recovered from the subsequent drop in water pressure, and the Great Seattle Fire destroyed thirty-one blocks.

Seattle's city leaders of the day showed unusual foresight, and instead of rebuilding what had been destroyed, they made two strategic decisions: to construct all new buildings of stone or brick to insure against a similar disaster in the future; and to regrade the streets one to two stories higher than the original street grade.

During the regrade, the streets were lined with concrete walls that formed narrow alleyways between the walls and the buildings on both sides of the street, with a wide canal where the street was. In the beginning, pedestrians climbed ladders to go between street level and the sidewalks in front of the building entrances. Brick archways were erected next to the road surface above the submerged sidewalks, which had skylights with small panes of clear glass, forming the area now called the Seattle Underground.

Pedestrians, however, continued to use the underground sidewalks that were illuminated by the glass prism skylights inserted at grade level in the sidewalks above and that are still seen on some streets. Then the threat of bubonic plague in 1907 forced city officials into condemning the underground city, just two years before Seattle would host the World's Fair of 1909. The basements of those buildings were left to deteriorate or were used as storage. Some became illegal flophouses for the homeless, gambling halls, speakeasies, and opium dens during the "Roaring Twenties."

Only a small portion of the Seattle Underground had been restored, making it safe and accessible to the public on guided tours.

It was here that Denise was instructed to meet with President Christophe's chief of staff after the tour had closed shop for the night and all the tourists had gone. She studied the subterranean environment as she waited. The president was in Seattle for a fundraising event, and Peter wanted to discuss a future endeavor that would require her skills, even though there was some question about her failure in Venezuela. It was not the first time she had met with Peter Abercrombie in hidden-away places. And although she was stopped by a couple of Secret Service agents as she was about to slip into the entrance with the picked lock, she had yet to see the chief of staff himself. Her guard was down, considering the quick meeting with the Secret Service men stationed by the door outside, so she did not hear the approach of the predator behind her.

She heard a throaty whisper in her ear: "Hello, my pretty."

She turned quickly and reached for a gun that was not there. The Secret Service agent had relieved her of her weapon when she came in. At the time it did not seem odd, as it had happened before. After all, she was not an employee of the government, and she had not been given any security clearances. Added to that was Peter's extreme paranoia.

Ezekiel laughed at her dilemma. "My, my, my, not as clever as you thought."

"But the Secret Service—" Denise choked out.

"Who said they were Secret Service? That's the problem with feeling too secure in your relationships. They often leave you vulnerable."

"You waited a long time to seek your revenge, Ezekiel, and you went to considerable trouble to arrange this little get-together. I'm surprised that Koshka didn't come herself. How did you ever get Peter to go along with this?" As she talked, Denise looked for anything that she could use as a weapon. A quick scan of Ezekiel's body showed no telltale signs of a gun. But surely he had not come here unarmed.

"The Russians have a saying: 'For a mad dog, seven versts is not a long detour'; in other words, time is on the side of the determined." Ezekiel turned his back to Denise as he fingered the large, oversized, ornate crucifix on a leather lace around his neck. "Peter was only too happy for you to disappear after your dismal performance in Venezuela. And I seldom allow someone else the pleasure of an activity I enjoy doing myself."

"Will the mad dog keep her hands clean and let her men do her dirty work?" Denise shrieked as she lunged for Ezekiel with a two-by-four she had quickly grabbed from a small pile of debris left behind by some past workers.

Ezekiel ducked as the two-by-four came whistling over his head. At the same time, he yanked on the crucifix. As the leather strap around his neck came loose, he pulled the top of the crucifix from a sheath, revealing a small but lethal dagger. He spun to face Denise and plunged the dagger into the woman's stomach. Grabbing her by the throat with his other hand, he pushed her backward until Denise's back was against the wall.

Ezekiel leaned forward and placed his lips on Denise's forehead. "I like to do my own killing," he said softly.

"Bastard," Denise choked out as blood started to trickle from her lips.

As he slowly moved the dagger upward, creating a large slice in the abdomen, Ezekiel dragged his lower lip on the female assassin's forehead in a slow, almost sexual way.

"Purify me with hyssop, Lord, and I shall be clean of sin," Ezekiel whispered in Denise's ear. "Wash me, and I shall be whiter than snow. Have mercy on me, God, in your great kindness. Purify me with hyssop, Lord, and I shall be clean of sin. Wash me, and I shall be whiter than snow."

It would be the last words Denise would ever hear as her body slipped to the dirty floor. Ezekiel crouched down beside her body and wiped the dagger on the dead woman's clothes. "I like this place. It has many ghosts to keep you company."

As Ezekiel came out the door onto the street, he nodded at the two men who were casually leaning up against the wall. They returned the nod and disappeared back through the door he had just come out of.

Ezekiel turned and walked a couple of blocks to the parking garage where a car was waiting for him. Once in the car, he retrieved a throwaway phone and dialed the number to the president's chief of staff.

"I thought you said she would meet me," Ezekiel demanded as soon as he heard the phone pick up. "You said you had it all arranged."

Peter Abercrombie seemed flustered at first as he stuttered one-syllable responses. Finally, he gained his composure. "She agreed to be there. She thought she was meeting me. I don't know—maybe she got suspicious. I did my part, though. I kept my end of the deal."

"Don't worry, Peter, your special proclivities are safe."

Peter heard a click, signaling that Ezekiel had hung up.

The sun was shining, and it was going to be a gorgeous day in Seattle as the first underground tour of the day started down the stairs into the abandoned city below. The tour guide was speaking about how the space under Seattle was often rented out for special occasions. Several teenage boys were pushing one another as they joked about their surroundings.

"You guys check it out. This would be a great place to bury a body."

Twenty-Eight

The next day Peter Abercrombie returned to his home in Falls Church, Virginia, oblivious to the death of his favorite hired gun. Ezekiel's presence had made the chief of staff so edgy that he had imbibed copious amounts of scotch to steady his nerves. His wife, Christina, lingered in the study, watching his descent into excess with disgust on her face.

Christina Abercrombie might have been married to the president's chief of staff, but she felt no loyalty to him. She had discovered many years ago that his cold, suspicious view of the world excluded any hope that they would enjoy the partnership that most couples enjoyed in a political marriage. His philandering with underage girls, combined with his extreme paranoia, put an end to any marital relationship after the birth of their youngest son. She had indulged her physical needs in short-term affairs with politically connected married men who wouldn't require any long-term commitment from her.

It was at a State Department function that she met Ezekiel Jones. He was charming and attentive to her. He had told her that he had seen her at other events and promised himself that at the first opportunity, he would make her acquaintance.

Though she knew nothing about him, she did notice that he was treated with deference by those who held the reins of power in Washington. Christina may have been cursed with a loveless marriage, but she was blessed with an abundance of political savvy. Polished and classy, the platinum blonde had won the hearts of the American people with her charitable work and her working-class background. Winning Ezekiel's agreement to join her in the bedroom was a small matter.

Under the public persona was a woman who was as ambitious as her husband, and she had big plans that did not include Peter. In fact, her endgame involved exposing her husband for the narcissist he was and playing on the sympathy votes she hoped to garner in a very public divorce proceeding to catapult her into a seat in the Senate. While the affair was short-lived, Ezekiel had become a type of mentor for her and showed her there was another way with the guarantee that she would emerge stronger, richer, and wield more influence. She was enlisted to aid a group of people who had so much power that it made her giddy—people who could make her a senator with a wave of their hands, people who showed their gratitude in a very generous manner to those who did them favors.

The calculating lady watched her husband sleep. He always slept on his back. Christina could never understand how that could be done. She always slept on her side. In yoga class, when they rested on their backs, the instructor referred to it as the "corpse shavasana pose."

The chief of staff looked like that. He looked as if he were lying on a coroner's table. The rhythm maintained by the rise and fall of his chest was stable and deep. Peter Abercrombie had taken a prescription sleeping pill prescribed by his personal physician. His paranoia, coupled with his obsessive-compulsive need to micromanage everything around him, would make sleeping soundly next to impossible if not for the help of the miracles of modern pharmaceuticals. The excitement of the event in Seattle the night before had faded quickly as the president's right-hand man settled in for the night.

She held the small syringe in her steady hands—hands that didn't even shake with the thought of the enormity of the action she was about to take.

The Abercrombie house was quiet, yet she knew that every room, every hallway, every nook had eyes that watched through cameras discreetly placed. Every room but this one. No one would ever think that the biggest threat to the president's chief of staff would be his wife.

However, Ezekiel was right—widows received much more sympathy than common divorcées. She had no doubt of the price she might pay if caught, but she of all people had the perfect opportunity, and the drug metabolized rapidly. She had done so much research before reaching this point.

Christina always prided herself on her attention to detail. It was a fixation that often drove those around her crazy, but now it left her feeling quite optimistic about her chances of success. She had been careful about using public computers whenever she snuck out without her husband being aware. It was easy enough to accomplish when she went home to visit her family. Her research revealed a poison called aconite as one of the strongest poisons known to man. Aconite was a plant indigenous to many parts of the world, and it was commonly used as an ornamental plant in North America. All parts of this plant were poisonous, but the root was the most toxic. The effects of a lethal dose were rapid, toxic symptoms showing themselves within a few moments. Ingestion of even a small amount resulted in severe gastrointestinal upset, but it was the effect on the heart, slowing it down until it stopped, that was often the cause of death.

Its historical name was wolfsbane, derived from the idea that arrows tipped with the juice, or baits anointed with it, would kill wolves. Half a tablespoon of a tincture of aconite root placed in a bottle of whisky was enough to kill a very large man. Aconite had been called "the perfect poison to mask a murder." It could be detected only by sophisticated toxicology analysis using equipment that was not always available to local forensic labs.

Creating a tincture from the aconite plant that she bought at a local fresh herb farm was also accomplished by a simple Google search.

The house was quiet. She was very light on her feet as she approached the bed and soundless as she slowly bent over Peter. He didn't even stir as the needle pricked the skin where his inner thigh joined the groin area. Very good sleeping pills indeed. She could only hope that the needle hole was small enough that, with it being in a skin fold, it would be overlooked by whoever performed the autopsy.

Christina watched her husband's sleeping form carefully, almost fearing to breathe. Her vigil was a short one, as within fifteen minutes, the chief of staff's body convulsed as the poison started running through his system. Christina observed her husband's hand clutching his chest. She felt a sudden and intense onset of anxiety. What if she didn't give him enough? What if he didn't die? She looked on as his skin turned a violent shade of red and felt warm when she reached out a curious hand to touch his skin. Even with the increasing warmth, he did not perspire. He started gasping for water as he was overcome by an unquenchable thirst for cold water. Christina didn't move from her spot as she watched with no emotion except for fear that he would live. Peter could feel a tingling sensation in his skin and excruciating pain in his joints; and his sight began to dim, but as it dimmed, he could see his wife sitting by his bed watching dispassionately, making no move to come to his aid. His pulse was weak and rapid, his pain acute. His heart began to beat wildly, erratically.

"Peter!" Christina screamed as she grabbed his shoulder. "Peter, my God what's wrong?"

Eyes filled with agony gazed at her in terror from a twisted face. He tried to speak but could not. His sight had completely abandoned him as he flayed about. His hearing failed, and although he had total consciousness, he was trapped in a silent dark cocoon as his body was racked by severe gastric and intestinal spasms, a headache besieged his skull, and the muscles in his body convulsed. Finally, Peter Abercrombie's pulse was imperceptible.

"Someone help me!" Christine screamed. "Help!"

Peter had been assigned protection by the Secret Service through the president's executive order. She scrambled onto the bed and, reaching under the night table, hit the panic button that would summon the Secret Service agent on the night shift. Although she had met the detail that protected them in the evening, she couldn't remember their names. She had seldom any reason to interact with them because she was either at an event or in bed.

It took only seconds for the first agent to burst through their bedroom door.

"My husband!" Christina screamed. "Please help him."

The agent turned to Christina.

"Call nine one one. Tell them we need an ambulance," he ordered. His calm voice filled the room, but his face betrayed the crisis he now faced. "I think he's having a heart attack."

Twenty-Nine

Koshka curled up on her couch. The events of the past few days had left her feeling quite satisfied. Feeling particularly hawkish tonight, she flipped on Fox News. She watched as Megan Kelly was interrupted by breaking news.

"President Bernard Christophe's chief of staff, Peter Abercrombie was rushed to the nearest hospital just after one this morning after suffering a severe heart attack. The man who holds more sway over the president than any other advisor lapsed into a coma while in the ambulance and has not regained consciousness."

The well-groomed male announcer spoke gravely. "We have been able to confirm that Christina Abercrombie has not left the hospital since the chief of staff was admitted and that immediate family members have been making arrangements to travel to the family's side. We will update you as we receive more information."

A small smile crept across her face as she flipped the channel to CNN. Their announcement was already in progress.

"The first family is asking for Americans to pray for the president's chief of staff, and people are gathering outside the hospital, holding a candlelight vigil. As we get more information, we will let our viewers know."

Funny, Koshka thought. The president was the first to promote separation of state and religion—in fact, the president often ridiculed the "faithful" for turning to God for salvation instead of the government. He had always wanted the government to replace God as the people's savior. An archaic communist thought. Let people keep their religion. Religious leaders could be bought. Now, though, the closet atheist was all in for prayers. This was one area where God will always trump government—at least in theory.

When Koshka woke up the following morning, she turned on CNN to hear that the first family and the Abercrombies were in mourning. Peter Abercrombie had passed on into nothingness. After all, if there is no God, there is no heaven, Koshka assumed.

The morning news anchor was solemn but conveyed some surprise that the newly widowed Christina Abercrombie would be addressing the country as soon as 3:00 p.m. *This should be good*, Koshka thought.

The news announcer turned the next story over to his picture-perfect sidekick, who attempted to look solemn and sexy at the same time.

"Officials from Colombia announced that they have found the badly decomposed remains of a man off a mountain road leading from Venezuela into Colombia. Investigators believe it is the remains of the former Venezuelan president, Gomez. Officials suspect that the former president lost control of his vehicle when he was fleeing the civil war in his country last year and perished in the accident. Sources close to the investigation say that they suspect that the reason it took so long to locate the remains is that the accident took place off a seldom-used dirt road in a remote area. The accident site was reported to local police in Cucuta, Colombia, by a farmer who stumbled on the scene while on his way to church. Questions still remain as to why President Gomez would have fled to Colombia, a country that has been historically aligned with the United States against the Venezuelan government."

All's well that ends well, Koshka thought. The discovery of the body did not concern her. She knew there would be nothing left that would point to foul play. Her people were professionals. The story did remind her of her best pitchman, though.

Andy's injuries in Venezuela had proven to be quite serious, and he was still restricted to working as the president of his garment workers' union—which, as far as the union was concerned, was good news. His absence while he was in a remote hospital facility operated by the CIA was explained away as a serious car accident while working with CUT, the union in Brazil, which required a fair amount of recuperation. The accident had taken place on a poorly maintained roadway on the side of a hill when Andy was on his way to give a speech to workers at a textile mill. No one from the union membership questioned this. Everyone knew the roads in South America were dangerous.

After Andy gained consciousness, Koshka asked him what had happened that day. Andy said that when he peered through the peephole to see if it really was room service that had knocked on the door, several bullets pierced the door. It was the last thing he remembered clearly. He did not remember the bullet biting into his chest, and he never saw the face of the person who pulled the trigger. He should have been more cautious. It wasn't until later, as the trauma receded and his memory returned, that he was able to recall more details about that night. And in recalling them, he was able to piece together that it was Dane and Marco who got his ass out of the hotel. He vaguely remembered a woman taking care of him, but he wasn't clear if that had really happened or if it was a creation of his fever-racked mind.

Koshka checked her messages and placed a call to Andy. He still had his feathers ruffled over being shot and the fact that no one had warned him from the beginning that he had a contract out on him. *He is such a prima donna*, Koshka thought.

Andy picked up on the third ring. He recognized the number on his caller ID and wanted to communicate to Koshka that he was still upset with the whole situation.

"Hello, Koshka," Andy answered.

"Good afternoon, Andy. How are you doing?" Koshka asked in her best conciliatory tone.

"Good. I would be doing better, though, if I had never been shot to begin with."

"Good Lord, Andy, you were shot *after* you knew. The information didn't help you at all. You still got your bloody ass shot off!"

"Actually, I was shot in the chest. My ass is fine."

"Yes, it is, or so I am told," Koshka said somewhat distantly as if her mind was somewhere else.

Andy smiled to himself. "So what do you have your claws into now?"

"Oh, nothing. Just thought I would see how you're doing and how you like running an actual union."

"It sucks," Andy griped. "Members are always complaining about corrupt union officials or saying that the union gave away the house in their labor agreements. They are always miserable. Someone is always wanting your job."

Koshka laughed. "Ah, the joys of responsibility."

"Which I try to avoid when I can."

There was a moment of silence; then Andy asked, "Have you moved into Cuba yet?"

"No, just setting it up now. Figuring out what the team will look like. It's an initial entry, so we're truly starting from scratch."

"You must be thinking of someone," Andy persisted.

"I'm thinking that Joyia might be perfect for this," Koshka shared.

"I will be ready in no time. I want in on Cuba."

"But I thought that you were at death's door. Now it's not a big deal?"

"I never said it wasn't a big deal. I just said that I have amazing recuperative powers, and I will be ready for Cuba."

"I think the ladies in your little garment union would miss you dreadfully," said Koshka. "I don't want to tear you away from the little darlings."

"Has anyone ever told you that you are a real bitch?"

Koshka laughed. "Andy, any woman can be a bitch. It's in her DNA. I, on the other hand, have always been an overachiever."

At that point Andy thought it would be safer to take the conversation in a different direction. When he asked about Marco and Francisco, Koshka responded that Marco had been in touch—in fact, he had asked about Andy's welfare. Marco was slated to hold a position in the new cabinet—secretary of commerce or some such thing. However, it was not until later that Francisco's body turned up among those who had died in the rioting several days later. Why he had returned to Caracas while it was still in the throes of reckless violence remained unclear, but he had sacrificed so much for their mission. He would be toasted as a patriot to Venezuela; and, as we all know, the tree of liberty required the blood of patriots.

Koshka made another note to herself to get a plaque put up in his memory. Not that she was sentimental, or even feeling a bit remorseful over his loss, but people would expect it.

Dane was still in Venezuela, helping the country transition into a part of what would someday be the New World. Things were going smoothly.

Thirty

Joyia had resurfaced in Oranjestad, the capital city of Aruba, several weeks after the top government officials in Venezuela had been jailed and the violence had abated enough for fresh leaders to emerge in the newly born democracy.

She had settled in at the Renaissance Aruba Resort and Casino for a little R&R and some adult playtime. This was not her first time to Aruba or the Renaissance. The rooms were modernly decorated, which suited her taste, and Joyia was always impressed with the cleanliness of every square inch of the grounds.

The resort also owned its own private island, Renaissance Island, giving Joyia the option to escape from people, if she chose to, by taking a water taxi to Aruba's only private beaches. Its unspoiled, isolated shores offered peace and privacy simply not found anywhere else in the world.

When she first arrived at the resort, Joyia spent many days there destressing from the chaos of the violence in Venezuela. Today, though, Joyia welcomed the company of humanity and the young, able-bodied men among the scores of tourists who converged at the hotel. For the past several days, she had limited herself to hanging out at the bar because of the extreme heat. The drinks were fabulous, the food was delicious, and the service was impeccable, so she had not minded the limitation on her beach time.

But now that the heat wave had broken, she had migrated to the beach and occupied one of those amazing circular lounges the resort had placed here and there on the sand. For the past few months, she had immersed herself in a book that Andy had given her when they first met up in Boa Vista. The book was about George Meany, Jay Lovestone, and the beginning of what would become the CLU. It was called *The Unspoken Legacy*.

She cracked open the book and started reading. After an hour spent studying the intricacies and political intrigue of the US government post–World War II, Joyia could no longer concentrate on what she was reading as the sound of the waves beckoned to her.

Joyia closed the book and laid it carefully on the blanket beside her. CLU was a different breed of organization from the original that started in a post–World War II world. Where it once was just content with eliminating communism, it had now expanded itself into embracing a one-world governance under the leadership of NATO, not the UN. Joyia, like most people, wanted to be on the winning side. In her mind, the winning side was CLU.

As she lounged on one of the beautiful beaches that Aruba was renowned for, her phone rang. She was greeted by the voice of Koshka Whitehall with an invitation to immediately come to Washington, DC. She had a job for the sultry South American, but she wouldn't discuss it over the phone. She said little when she called. She seldom said much over the phone anyway, even phones that were secured. She simply told Joyia that she was needed.

Of course, Joyia made travel arrangements immediately. She would be flying out tomorrow. Aruba would have to get along without her for now.

"Are you sure NED is moving on Venezuela?" she asked him as she toyed with the ring on her pinkie finger. The band was inlaid with fire opals that displayed bright, vibrant colors. White-gold lines cut through the opal, creating a geometric pattern around the band. At the top of the band was the letter V, created with diamond pave.

"Of course," he answered, very sure of himself and his knowledge.

"We should let them move forward," she said. "Venezuela is no friend to us, but eventually we'll have to start the transition. Eventually NED and CLU will have to take down the US government for us."

"Of course. But we have to be careful how we proceed. The Board wants to move on to Cuba next. If they even have a hint that we have infiltrated CLU and NED…" He didn't need to finish his sentence. She knew the ramifications. Their movement's survival depended on doing this right.

"We let them take out our enemies as we slowly take them over," she responded.

Ezekiel smiled as he hung up the phone. There were so many sides to play in this game, and he loved playing each of them. Yes, he thought, the best part of the game was still to come.

END

Appendix

The creation of NED and its coconspirator Solidarity Center were hardly the beginning of the alliance between organized labor and the US government. To understand that, one would have to visit World War II and the AFL (prior to its merger with the CIO) that created a partnership with the CIA to stop the influx of communism into the trade unions of Europe as they started to rebuild themselves in the aftermath of the war.

George Meany and Jay Lovestone were introduced by David Dubinsky, president of the International Ladies' Garment Workers' Union (ILGWU), in October 1941, shortly after Meany had become secretary-treasurer of the AFL. Dubinsky, Lovestone's benefactor, told Meany, "The son of a bitch is OK. He's been converted." With that statement, a partnership was formed that would bind the two men together over three decades. At times it was an uneasy partnership, but it survived despite the strong egos both men possessed, and it created a new world on two continents—perhaps more—that reporters would never report, and history books would never fully record.

George's views were built on union philosophy and colored with a heavy dose of red, white, and blue. George loved the United States.

During World War II, he was one of the permanent representatives of the AFL to the National War Labor Board. George Meany had become an anticommunist zealot. His view of the world was simple: communists were the great devils, and the struggle against communism took precedence over domestic affairs and even over labor issues. In 1945, he spear-headed the AFL boycott of the World Federation of Trade Unions because they welcomed participation by Communist labor groups from the Soviet Union. It was during this time that he established close ties to prominent anticommunists in the US labor movement.

Young Jacob Liebstein was spellbound by Socialist politics from his teens and absorbed all the ideological undercurrents in the vibrant New York Yiddish and English radical press.

In February of 1919, the young immigrant dramatically changed the path of his mundane life. He started by changing his name, Jacob Liebstein, to Jay Lovestone, and then followed that by becoming a full-fledged member of the Communist Party.

Lovestone became editor of the Communist Party news-paper in 1921, which had been simply titled *The Communist*. In keeping with his penchant for the printed word, he was on the editorial board of *The Liberator*, an arts and letters pub-lication of the Workers' Party of America. Upon the death of Charles Ruthenberg in 1927, he became the Communist Party's national secretary. Sometime in 1923, the Communist Party of America developed two main factions: the Pepper-Ruthenberg bloc and the Foster-Cannon bloc. Lovestone was a close supporter of the Pepper-Ruthenberg leaning, which was to be centered in New York City and to favor united-front political action in a "class Labor Party."

With the Soviet Bolshevik party fragmented by a suc-cession brawl following Lenin's death in January 1924, the political factions in the CPA began creating alliances with the political factions in the Soviet leadership. Foster's faction aligned itself with Joseph Stalin. Lovestone's faction was not as astute in its choice of political allies, as it was sympathetic to Nikolai Bukharin.

When Stalin removed Bukharin from the Soviet Politburo in 1929, Lovestone suffered the consequences of a poor political partnership. In the same spirit as his move to eliminate Cannon from political power, his rival William Z. Foster smelled blood in the water and assumed his position as party secretary when a visiting delegation of the Comintern asked him to step down.

Jay Lovestone was not one to give up what was his without a fight. He refused and promptly departed for the Soviet Union to appeal his case. Lovestone argued that he had the loyalty of an overwhelming majority of the Communist Party and should not be forced to step down.

Upon returning to the United States, Lovestone felt the full vengeance of Stalin for his lack of obedience, his alliance with Bukharin and the Right Opposition, and for his theory of American exceptionalism, which held that "capitalism was more secure in the United States and thus Socialists should pursue different, more moderate strategies there than elsewhere in the world." Lovestone's theories refuted Stalin's vision and the new Third-Period policy of ultra-leftism endorsed by the Comintern. Lovestone was expelled from the party—allegedly not for challenging Stalin but rather for his ill-fated allegiance to Stalin's opponent.

While still in the good graces of the Communist Party, Jay Lovestone had been an active participant in the party's labor undertakings, mainly within the United Mine Workers, where the party supported the rebellion headed by John Brophy against John L. Lewis's governance. His allies within the party, particularly Charles S. Zimmerman, had a great deal of power within the ILGWU prior to the debacle of 1926. It was the same union that Meany's wife, Eugenie, was a member of. After his expulsion, Lovestone formed a base within ILGWU Dressmakers Local 22, to which Zimmerman had returned after his expulsion from the CPUSA. Lovestone and Zimmerman worked their way into the good graces of ILGWU President David Dubinsky, who had been their fiercest enemy before their expulsion.

Jay Lovestone finally found his niche in the world of revolutions at the age of forty-one. His obsession was to eliminate communists from the American labor movement, and he was a driven man.

Success was not to be had for young Lovestone within the true confines of the labor movement—especially the CIO, which had its share of Communist Party loyalists. They had no room for a CP reject.

The United States rose from the ashes of World War II tougher than ever, but Europe was not so lucky. It was devastated both physically and economically. The Marshall Plan gave the key leadership role to the United States regarding the rebuilding of the Western European economies utilizing the United States' newfound financial and military strength. The Marshall plan would usher in a period of robust recovery for Europe, but it would also usher in the cold war between the two new superpowers—the United States and the USSR.

It was President Harry Truman who reached out to the AFL to deal with the more radically communist elements that were at work in Europe to subvert democracy and the rebuilding of Europe. Under the leadership of the AFL, American union representatives would deal with the left-leaning communist labor groups who were committed to the subjugation of Europe to the Communist Party. The AFL leaders answered the call of President Truman, and they were ready and willing.

Matthew Woll, president of the photoengravers union and one of the four labor leaders on the AFL's Free Trade Union Committee, wrote Frank Wisner, a top officer of the CIA: "This is to introduce Jay Lovestone…He is duly authorized to cooperate with you on behalf of our organization and to arrange for close contact and reciprocal assistance in all matters."

But it was James Angleton who turned Jay Lovestone's direction and political agenda. It was Angleton who gave Jay Lovestone a purpose—a purpose backed by the CIA. Angleton's career in the CIA spanned decades and spawned many conspiracy theories. Born in Boise, Idaho, in 1917, Angleton became renowned in later years as the only person to have been able to blackmail J. Edgar Hoover because of his homosexuality. Angleton arranged for Lovestone to become a senior figure within the ILGWU, where he started identifying Communist Party members, who were once his friends, for Angleton.

In 1944, Lovestone was placed on the AFL's Free Trade Union Committee, where he worked out of the ILGWU's headquarters. Along with Irving Brown, he led the activities of the American Institute for Free Labor Development, an organization sponsored by the AFL that worked internationally, organizing free labor unions in Europe and Latin America, which were not communist-controlled.

These two were to carry their crusading anticommunism against the growing strength of the left in the European labor movements. Irving Brown would eventually receive the Congressional Medal of Honor from President Ronald Reagan.

With a letter written on December 10, 1948, the AFL began a relationship with the CIA that was to endure through the following decades and into the present day.

The appropriateness of an American labor movement becoming the apparatus or other half of a government intelligence agency was completely satisfactory to the Meany-Dubinsky-Woll triad, as long as it was in the service of an anticommunist struggle and the defeat of communist-led unions. Furthermore, no US union leader ventured to defy the clandestine, quid-pro-quo relationship between organized labor and the international organization of espionage.

As secretive as the contact was between the AFL and the CIA, the one forged between the CIO and the CIA was even more so. The AFL and the Congress of Industrial Organizations (CIO) were not originally one organization. In fact, the two held a deep dislike for each other. The AFL was made up of skilled tradespeople, such as masons and carpenters. They considered themselves superior to the unskilled factory workers that made up the CIO. It was Thomas Braden, the assistant to CIA director Allan Dulles, who came to be the intermediary between the CIO and the CIA. Braden flew to Detroit to deliver $50,000 in cash to Walter Reuther, the UAW president, who was only too happy to receive it.

One would be hard-pressed to find any public record of how much financial incentive the CIA gave both labor movement organizations. There was no congressional oversight of the agency. As Thomas Braden once said: "The CIA could do exactly as it pleased. It could buy armies. It could buy bombs. It was one of the first worldwide multinationals."

In the face of plenty of proof to the contrary, Meany, Dubinsky, and Woll vowed to their dying day that not one of them—or Lovestone or even the AFL—were entangled in any way with the CIA. It would have been, and still would be, an outrageous scandal that would probably have ruined them as labor leaders, and consequently destroyed the labor organization, if it had been made public that they had not only collaborated with the CIA but also had accepted cash from the intelligence agency to advance its agenda.

The CIA made sure that no evidence of the money paid ever reached the labor giant's headquarters in Washington or that Meany got even a penny of it, but the fact that Lovestone functioned as a CIA operative with Meany's approval is beyond question.

It wasn't until 1955 that the AFL would merge with the CIO, creating the AFL-CIO—a merger, some believed, that was orchestrated by the CIA. By this time most militant left-wing leaders had been expelled from the CIO, enabling George Meany to effectively promote his anticommunist ideology.

In 1963 Lovestone became director of the AFL-CIO's international affairs department (IAD). In this post he sent millions of dollars from the CIA to aid anticommunist activities internationally, particularly in Latin America. It was referred to as the Lovestone Empire.

For nearly thirty years, George Meany, a New Yorker who rose to be the undisputed leader of the American labor movement, collaborated with Jay Lovestone. The odd partnership between the portly, cigar-chomping Meany and the slender Jewish man with the high cheekbones and hawkish nose would span several presidencies. It was a powerful combination: the strong-willed labor leader, who was on first-name terms with every US president from Franklin D. Roosevelt to Ronald Reagan; and Lovestone, a crafty, single-minded, behind-the-scenes operator, who had hands-on experience about what was going on, not only in the Soviet Union but also in Western Europe. Their ambitious plan to build an international network of pro-democracy unions that were under their control launched a global complex that not only survived but has thrived, right down to the present day.

When the chair of the Senate Foreign Relations Committee, Charles Percy (Republican, Illinois), introduced legislation creating the National Endowment foundation in the US Senate, he stated that he thought that the legislation was "arguably the most important single US foreign-policy initiative of this generation."

The tragedy of 9/11 spurred the NED board of directors to espouse its third strategic document. With the creation of this third document came funding for countries that had now attracted the attention of the US government and its military complex. The special funding NED received was targeted toward countries with large Muslim populations and countries located in the Middle East, Africa, and Asia.

NED's status as an NGO had a number of benefits that were known by those governmental bodies that really did carry out American foreign policy. A letter signed by seven former secretaries of state in 1995 (James Baker, Laurence Eagleburger, George Schultz, Alexander Haig, Henry Kissinger, Edmund Muskie, and Cyrus Vance) acknowledged the advantages an organization like NED offered in assisting the United States in promoting its foreign policy: "We consider the nongovernmental character of the NED even more relevant than it was at NED's founding twelve years ago.

In his 2004 book, *In Support of Democratization: Free Trade Unions and the Destabilization of Autocratic Regimes*, Joseph Siedlecki advocated "soft power," the need for a "more nuanced approach" to spreading democracy: "As an aspect of soft power, the United States should dramatically increase support for labor movements and free trade unions in developing countries."

In some campaigns, especially those involving the former USSR, the union has proved to be an advocate for democracy, as it was in Poland in 1989 and Czechoslovakia in 1990. In Spain in 1977, unions played a role that resulted in democratically elected leadership. But in South Africa, the involvement took a different turn. In South Africa apartheid had deeply established roots, and at the beginning of the revolts to overthrow apartheid, the AFL-CIO strongly opposed the antiapartheid unions. The opposition lasted until 1986, when it became apparent that a different and more intelligent tactic was vital. Whatever the particulars of the situation, it is clear that top-level foreign-policy officials in and around the US government see trade unions and labor movements as key allies in their efforts to maintain and expand US interests.

There is substantial proof that AFL-CIO foreign operations have worked hand-in-hand with the CIA. This shrouded approach has proven that labor's foreign policy and its resulting foreign operations are not only funded overwhelmingly by the government but have been advanced within, and are under the auspices of, officials at top levels of the AFL-CIO.

Many from the labor movement—including the now-deceased Irving Brown, Tom Kahn, Lane Kirkland, and Jay Lovestone, as well as others who still live—have been and remain members of a select but very influential assemblage of individuals who are still in or who have been a part of the US labor movement, who maneuver within a complex of reactionary political societies that work to promote sociopolitically created foreign-policy objectives from their lofty union positions.

The number of high-level AFL-CIO leaders who have been invited into and have joined top-level US foreign-policy circles and actively participated in US foreign-policy initiatives without informing their affiliated unions and their members, much less asking for a mandate to do so, remain a mystery. The leaders of the AFL-CIO have consciously kept these affiliations a secret.

Research

Articles:

Kelber, Harry. "AFL is Funded for Covert Activity by CIA In Long-Standing Ties with Spy Agency."

Books:

Alba, Victor. *Politics and the Labor Movements in Latin America*. Stanford, CA: Stanford Univ. Press, 1968.

Alexander, Robert J. *Organized Labor in Latin America*. New York: The Free Press, 1965.

Aronowitz, Stanley. *False Promises: The Shaping of American Working Class Consciousness*. New York: McGraw Hill, 1973.

Boyce, Richard O., and Herbert M. Morals. *Labor 1: An Untold Story*. New York: United Electrical Workers, 3rd Ed., 1972.

Dulles, Foster, Rhea. *Labor in America, a History*. New York: Thomas Y. Crowell Co., 1960.

Foner, Philip S. *American Labor and the Indochina War: The Growth of Union Opposition*. New York: International Publishers, 1971.

Foster, William Z. *Outline History of the World Trade Union Movement*. New York: International Publishers, 1956.

Galeano, Eduardo. *The Open Veins of Latin America.* Translated by Cedrie Belfrage. 3 Monthly Review, 1973.

Gerassi, John. *The Great Fear in Latin America* (6th printing). New York: Collier Books, 1971.

Godard, Eduardo Lab area, Chile Inuadido, Santiago, Editor an Austral, 1969.

Gompers, Samuel. *Seventy Years of Life and Labor.* New York: E. P. Dutton & Co., 1943.

Hawkins, Carroll. *Two Democratic Labor Leaders in Conflict! The Latin American Revolution and the Role of the Workers.* Lexington, MA: Lexington Books, 1973.

Levenstein, Harvey A. *Labor Organisations in the United States and Mexico.* Westport, CT: Greenwood Publishing Co., 1971.

Lieuwen, Edwin. *Arms and Politics in Latin America.* New York: Fraeger, 1967.

Light, Robert E., and Carl Marzani. *Cuba vs. the CIA.* New York: Marzani & Munsell, 1961.

Lipset, Seymour M., Martin Trow, and James Coleman. *Union Democracy: The Internal politics of the International Typographical Union.* Garden City: Doubleday Anchor, 1956.

Mader, Julius. *Who Is Who in the CIA*. Berlin: Mader, 1968.

McCoy, Alfred W. *The Politico of Heroin in Southeast Asia*. New York: Harper & Row, 1972.

McGreevy, Patrick J. *CIA, the Myth and the Madness*. Baltimore: Penguin Books, 1972.

Mills, C. Wright. *Power Politics and People*. New York: Ballantries, 1963.

Morris, George. *The CIA and American Labor*. New York: International, 1967.

Petras, James, and Maurice Zeitlin. *Latin Americas: Reform or Revolution? A Reader*. New York: Fawcett, 1969.

Radosh, Ronald. *American Labor and United States Foreign Policy*. New York: Random House, 1969.

Romualdi, Serafino. *Presidents and Peons*. New York: Funk & Wagnalls, 1967.

Smith, Richard Harris. *OSS: The Secret History of America & First Central Intelligence Agency*. Berkeley, CA: Univ. of California Press, 1972.

Sturmthal, Adolf, and James G. Scoville. *The International Labor Movement in Transition*. Urbana, IL: Univ. of Illinois Press, 1973.

Wimdmuller, John P. *International Trade Union Organisations: Structure, Functions and Limitations.* New York: Harper & Row, 1967.

Zink, Dolph Warren. *The Political Risks for Multinational Corporations in Developing Countries.* New York: Praeger, 1973.

Periodicals:

Berger, Henry W. "American Labor Overseas." *The Nation* (January 1967).

Bodenheimer, Susan. "The AFL-CIO in Latin America—The Dominican Republic: A Case Study." *Viet Report* (September–October 1967).

"U.S. Labor's Conservative Role in Latin America." *The Progressive November* (1967).

Braden, Thomas W., "I'm Glad the CIA is Immoral." *Saturday Evening Post* (May 1967).

Grace, J. Peter. "Labor Group Boosts Living Standards." *The Journal of Commerce* (April 1966).

Jerome, Gail S. "American Labor in Latin America. *Cross Currents* XXI, no. iii (1971).

Kurzman, Dan. "Labor's Cold Warrior." *Washington Post*, December 30, 1965.

"Lovestone's Cold War." *The New Republic* (June 1966).

Lens, Sidney. "Lovestone Diplomacy." *The Nation* (July 1965).

"Labor between Bread and Revolution." The Nation (September 1966).

North American Congress on Latin America [NACLA]. "Latin America & Empire Report" (October 1973).

"New Chile." *NACLA* (1972).

Romualdi, Serafino. "The Latin Labor Leader—Democratic and Dedicated." *The American Federation* (April 1964).

Simons, Marlise. "The Brazilian Connection." *Washington Post*, January 6, 1974.

TIME Magazine, September 24, IS 73.

Winship, North. "The American and the Confederate Avantis." October 16, 1918.

Unpublished Speeches and Papers

American Institute for Free Labor Development, 1962–1972. A Decade of Worker to Work Cooperation, Washington, DC.

The AXFLD Reporter, Washington, DC.

United States Senate, Committee on Foreign Relation Hearing on AIFLD with George Meany, August 1, 1969, Washington, DC, US Government Printing Office.

"Survey of the Alliance for Progress. Compilation of Studies and Hearings of Subcommittee on American Republic Affairs," April 29, 1969

Washington, DC, US Government Printing Office

Meany, George. "National Press Club Speech." Reprinted in congressional record, July 25, 1967, pp. H9370–72.

University of Chicago Research Center in Economic Development and Change. "United States–Latin American Relations. United States Business and Labor in Latin America." Study prepared at request of Subcommittee on American Republic Affairs, Committee on Foreign Relations. US Senate, Washington, DC, 1960.

[North Winship, "Gompers 1 Visit to Milan, Oct. 17, 191 fl.] *[Memo of Algie H. Simons, Gompers* Manuscripts, Sept, 12, 1918.] *[Julius Mader, "Who's Who in the CIA/ 1 p. 75, 318.] *[Sinclair Snow, "Samuel Gompers and the Pan American Federation of Labor," Doctoral Dissertation, UNV. of Virginia, i960, pp. 68–71.]

[Samuel Gompers, "Seventy Years of Life and Labor," pp. 321 * 512*]

www.ingramcontent.com/pod-product-compliance
Lightning Source LLC
Chambersburg PA
CBHW051419170626
46809CB00006B/2226